DEAD LOUDMOUTH

DEAD LOUDMOUTH

VICTORIA HOUSTON

Published by
TYRUS BOOKS
an imprint of F+W Media, Inc.
10151 Carver Road, Suite 200
Blue Ash, OH 45242. U.S.A.
www.tyrusbooks.com

Hardcover ISBN 10: 1-4405-6845-6
Hardcover ISBN 13: 978-1-4405-6845-9
Paperback ISBN 10: 1-4405-6844-8
Paperback ISBN 13: 978-1-4405-6844-2
eISBN 10: 1-4405-6846-4
eISBN 13: 978-1-4405-6846-6

Printed in the United States of America.

10 9 8 7 6 5 4 3 2 1

Library of Congress Cataloging-in-Publication Data
Houston, Victoria, author.
Dead loudmouth / Victoria Houston.
Blue Ash, OH: Tyrus Books, [2016] | Series: Loon Lake mystery series
LCCN 2015047504 (print) | LCCN 2016001975 (ebook) | ISBN 9781440568459 (hc) | ISBN 1440568456 (hc) | ISBN 9781440568442 (pb) | ISBN 1440568448 (pb) | ISBN 9781440568466 (ebook) | ISBN 1440568464 (ebook)
LCSH: Ferris, Lewellyn (Fictitious character)—Fiction. | Osbourne, Doc (Fictitious character)—Fiction. | Policewomen—Wisconsin—Fiction. | Murder—Investigation—Fiction. | Kidnapping—Investigation—Fiction. | BISAC: FICTION / Mystery & Detective / Women Sleuths. | GSAFD: Mystery fiction.
LCC PS3608.O88 D4357 2016 (print) | LCC PS3608.O88 (ebook) | DDC 813/.6—dc23
LC record available at *http://lccn.loc.gov/2015047504*

Cover design by Stephanie Hannus.
Cover image © iStockphoto.com/LawrenceSawyer.

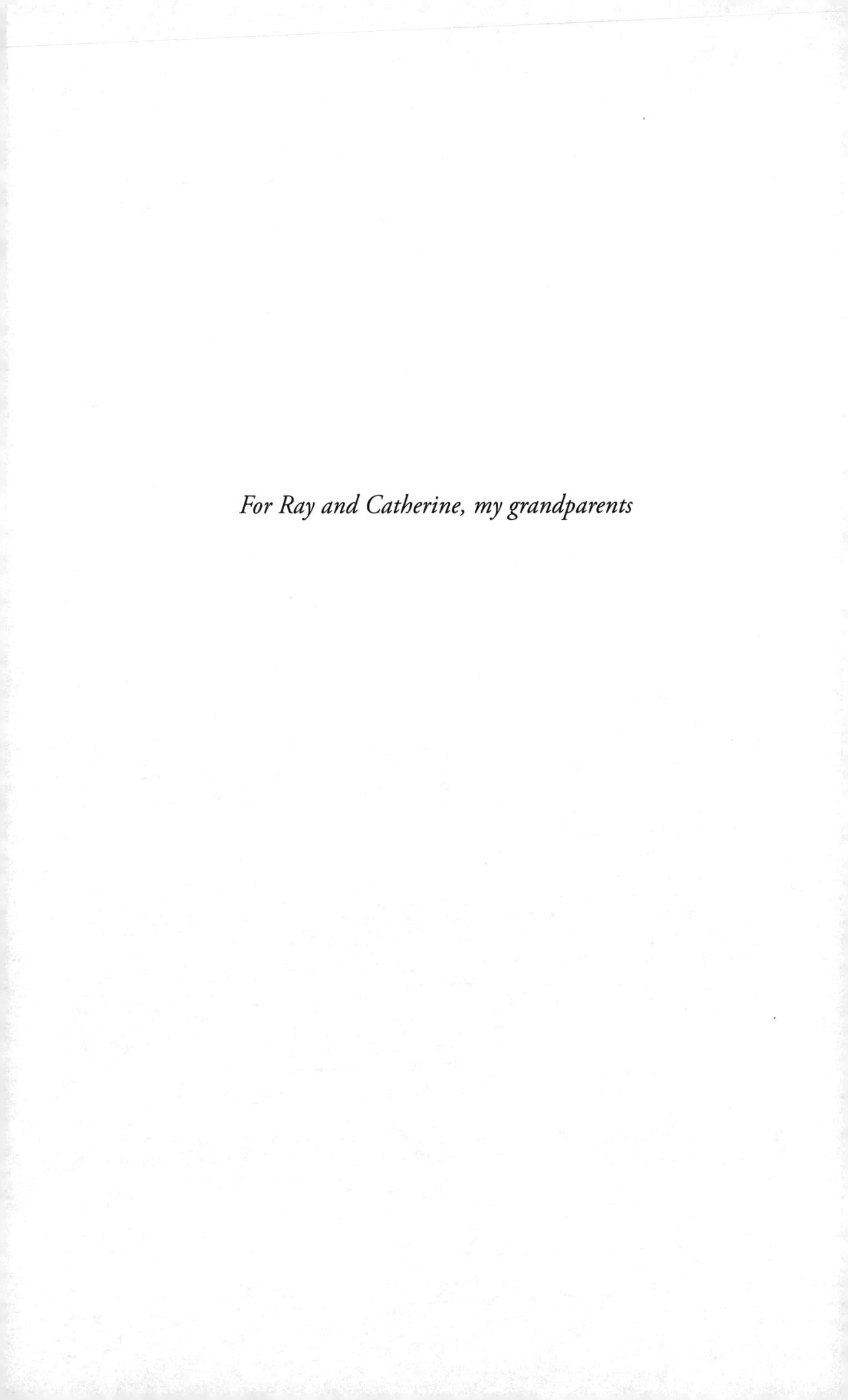

For Ray and Catherine, my grandparents

"A high station in life is earned by the gallantry with which appalling experiences are survived with grace."

—TENNESSEE WILLIAMS

Chapter One

The owl, poised still as a rock on his favorite perch, the broken branch of the old oak tree, scanned the ground below still hoping for a late dinner. Alerted to the sound of an approaching intruder, he tipped his elegant head to one side as the creature invaded his territory. Neither deer nor bear nor raccoon, the shadowy shape resembled none of his usual prey traveling the deer trail. The owl stared, confident his burning eyes would terrorize the unwitting trespasser.

To his surprise he was ignored. Ignored and unseen, he chose to watch.

Rocking back and forth as it bumped forward in low gear, a golf cart made its way over the roots and rocks sabotaging the path worn by bears addicted to the garbage spilling from bins behind the supper club. Ah, now the owl understood: this was one of those who hunted in the sunlight.

After parking in a clearing off to the side of honeysuckle planted to mask the garbage from the parking lot, the driver turned off the ignition and waited, listening.

Except for the excitement of birds thrilled that the sun had just peeked over the pines lining the eastern shore of the lake . . . no other sounds.

Stepping off the cart the driver hurried past the bins to the rear of the building then stopped to listen again before moving forward. But the only sound besides the birds was a faint squish of sand and leaves underfoot where the ground was soggy from a downpour two days earlier. Yet the watcher in the tree heard what the intruder did not: leaves whispering in an early morning breeze, waves lapping softly on the shore beyond the woods.

As the owl watched, the hunter pursued its prey.

The window the driver had jimmied open the night before was still ajar—enough that one shove pushed it wide open, but a quick glance inside didn't help: no sightline to the stage. The driver knew the answer to that problem. The Formica-topped workbench just inside the open window would make for easy access without having to use the front door.

Pushing away the dusty curtain that had been hung in front of the window to discourage curious teenage boys, the driver crawled in far enough to perch, knees bent, on the countertop. The driver waited, breath held. No sound.

From that angle the underside of the white baby grand piano was in full sight. A man's foot could be seen sticking out over the top edge of the piano but there was no sign of the woman. The foot was still; not even a toe moved.

Satisfied, the driver backed out of the window, dropping feet first onto the ground. Scraping over half-buried rocks, the golf cart wheeled in a tight circle to start back on the path. Less than a hundred yards away was the snowmobile trail that ran between the county highway, the woods, and the lake.

Mission accomplished, thought the driver. In less than an hour I can reach the car, get to the cabin, change clothes, and be back at Deer Creek with no one the wiser. So sorry, Miss Niedermeier, you should have thought before you spoke.

As the cart bounced in the direction of the snowmobile path, one set of eyes was still watching. Yellow, unblinking eyes. Eyes that could never bear witness because a snowy owl is soundless, except when breeding.

Chapter Two

Checking her watch, Loon Lake's chief of police picked up her stride as she wove her way, smiling, through clusters of youngsters chatting, skipping, and being flat-out noisy on their way to summer fun—swimming lessons, soccer practice, summer school—wherever they were going, spirits were high. Had to be. The day was sunny, the breeze light, and the air fragrant with the scent of mock orange.

"Lewellyn, this is damn good," the mayor had said moments earlier after running his finger down her spreadsheet of misdemeanors committed over the holiday weekend. "No felony assaults, no burglaries—not even a DUI? *Very good news.* You know, this will make for a terrific banner on the Chamber's new website." He nodded with enthusiasm as he spoke.

"I may write it myself: 'Visit Loon Lake—Your Haven for Big Fish and Family Fun.' Hell, this could be just what we need to get a Target up here. Excellent work, Chief Ferris. You are making all of us look good."

Lew had given him a tight smile. She was not going to argue. If he was happy, she was happy. Too often life in the Northwoods wasn't so benign. And when that happened whose fault was it? Law enforcement's? Or was it having a woman as the chief of police?

She was so used to seeing the latter question on the mayor's face that she was relieved to start this week with the guy in a better humor, even if they both knew that while Loon Lake might be felony-free for the moment, it was a hotbed of hunting and fishing violations. But that was not her worry or his: the game wardens would have to handle those bad actors.

Lew picked up her pace as the busy downtown streets gave way to the quiet, tree-lined boulevard leading to the old brownstone courthouse where the jail and the police station were housed. She could hear the scream of a Jet Ski speeding along the river that wound through town. Ah, summer in full swing.

Her office was welcoming with the midmorning sun spilling through the tall windows lining the south and west walls. A quick glance at the coffeepot in the corner showed at least two cups remaining—and still hot.

"Lew, got a minute?" She was in the midst of pouring her penultimate cup of coffee when she heard a voice that had a way of making her smile. "I can come back if you're busy," said Dr. Paul Osborne from the doorway.

"No, Doc, come on in. If you behave, I'll let you have my last cup of coffee . . ."

"If I *behave*?" Osborne glanced behind him to be sure no one else was walking in. "That's asking a lot." He grinned as he bent to give her quick kiss. "Sorry to intrude, Lew. I know you have meetings this morning, but I was just over at Erin's," he said, referring to his youngest daughter whose family lived kitty-corner to the courthouse, "and got a little piece of good news I'd like to share. Nothing too special, but it made my day—"

Before he could finish his sentence, the phone on Lew's desk rang simultaneously with the cell phone in the holster on her waist. She reached for the cell phone and looked down. "It's dispatch with an emergency—hold on, Doc. Damn, I knew the day was going too well . . ." She picked up the landline on her desk. "Marlaine? Sure . . . put him through."

"Chief, can you hear me?" A wheeze of a voice came crackling through the phone.

"Roger? Yes. You're breaking up a little but I can hear you okay. What's wrong?"

"Oh, man. We got a double something up on a piano here at Buddy's Place—that new gentlemen's club out on County Q?"

"Yep, right. I know where you mean and . . ."

"Two, Chief, and they are dead, real dead—"

"Have you called for an ambulance?"

"Yes, the EMTs are on their way but you have to call Pecore, too. I'm sure these folks are gone. I mean that's sure as hell how it looks to me and, Chief, it is *weird*—"

"Hold on, Roger," said Lew, interrupting the officer as she glanced over at Osborne. "Okay, I'm putting you on speaker. Doc Osborne is here so in case Pecore can't make it up there right away . . ."

She didn't have to add that any call to the Loon Lake coroner too early in the day was likely to catch him nursing a hangover, a hangover of such magnitude that more than once the man's shaky hands, limited knowledge of law enforcement protocol (or deliberate ignorance of such), and sloppy record keeping had combined with his alcohol-pickled brain cells to compromise an investigation. Only the fact that he was the mayor's brother-in-law saved his ass.

"And therein lies the problem of *appointed* public servants," Lew would mutter each time she had to find a way to work around the overserved jabone.

She hit the speaker button on her desk phone: "Okay, Roger, start from the beginning, please."

"Chief, we got two bodies—fragrant derelicts. Know what I mean?"

Lew looked over at Osborne, a puzzled expression on her face.

"I think he means 'in flagrante delicto,'" whispered Osborne, leaning forward in the chair in front of Lew's desk where he had seated himself after pouring the last cup of coffee. "That means naked and . . . ," he hesitated as he searched for a polite way to describe what he imagined Roger must mean, ". . . *entwined* for lack of a better word."

"Really?" whispered Lew, covering the mouthpiece of her phone. "How do you know *that*?"

"Six years of Latin in a Jesuit boarding school," said Osborne.

"Ah," said Lew with a nod as she dropped her hand from the phone. "So, Roger, I think you mean 'in flagrante delicto,' correct? Are the victims naked?"

"Yes, I've never seen anything like it. But then—"

"Get to the point, Roger. You have two naked people dead on a piano. Correct?"

"Yes, but up high."

"High? Now don't jump to conclusions. That'll require drug testing by the crime lab. I'll put a call in to the Wausau boys and let them—"

"No, Chief, that's not what I mean. The bodies are up high."

That was too much for Lew.

"Look, I'll check with Pecore and be right there. Take me fifteen, maybe twenty minutes. You secure the area. And, Roger, be sure to retrace your steps and do not touch anything. This could be an accident or it could be a crime scene so please be careful. Except for the EMTs be sure to keep people away from the site."

"Chief Ferris, I gotta tell you, I have never seen anything like this." The older officer was beside himself.

"Roger, please. Don't hyperventilate. Just settle down and do what I've asked you to. I'll be there shortly."

Hanging up, she looked over at Osborne. "Oh golly, Roger Adamczak, of all people to run into something like this. Honestly, Doc, I will bet you that man has never even seen his *wife* naked. Whatever he's run into out there at Buddy's Place, I'm lucky I haven't just lost one of my only two full-time officers to a heart attack."

Chapter Three

Lew was ten minutes down the road when she remembered that Osborne had mentioned he had good news he wanted to share. Oh darn. She had been in such a rush to get going she had forgotten to ask what that was. Sheesh, one more thing to ruin the day.

The most recent was that numnut Pecore picking up his phone instead of letting it go to voice mail. And, boy, did the day go downhill from there: Not only was he sober but a l-i-t-t-l-e too enthusiastic about meeting up at Buddy's Place.

"When was the last time that jabone was the least bit interested in showing up for the job he's paid to do?" she had asked Osborne after the call and before swallowing the last of her coffee. "Could it be he thinks he'll get free drinks and a front-row seat at a strip joint?" She shook her head in disgust. "I hate being right all the time."

Arriving at Buddy's Place, Lew pulled her cruiser alongside the ambulance, which was parked next to Roger's squad car. Two women and three men were standing in the shade of a large basswood tree off to one side of the parking lot, not far from a gravel walkway marking the entrance to the gentlemen's club. One of the men gave a polite wave as she stepped out of the car. Lew acknowledged the wave with a nod.

She wasn't surprised to see a crowd starting to gather. Even though cell service in the Northwoods is more fib than fact, cell phones are ubiquitous. Well aware of her elderly officer's short memory for department rules, she figured he had called one of his buddies in the area while waiting for her and that one call would have multiplied within seconds to homes up and down the county road. That plus the ambulance siren would have alerted any residents with time on their hands—or unpleasant chores—eager to see what all the excitement was.

Either that or the folks waiting under the tree were patrons. Lew had noticed on the Buddy's Place billboard, which she had passed moments earlier, that the club opened at noon six days a week ("closed Sundays"). But if they were patrons, they were at least an hour early.

She gave the group a quick once-over as she hurried toward the club entrance. Nope—no patrons in that crowd. They looked more like curious neighbors than people anxious for a midday break of booze and pole dancing. Plus they were staying a polite distance behind the yellow crime scene tape Roger had put up to close off the front of the building as well as half the parking area. Taping off a crime scene was one of the few things at which Roger excelled.

As Lew neared the building, the front door swung open and Roger stepped out to hold the door open so she could enter. "Follow me, Chief," he said, his voice low as if he thought the bystanders might hear too much. "Joe Teske is here with the EMTs. He's confirmed what I thought was the situation."

She walked into a hallway lined with windows on both sides, their white wooden shutters open to let the sun pour in. On the wall between the windows someone had hung framed antique beer posters. If she didn't know better, Lew would have thought she was walking into a classy restaurant.

"The janitor called in the alarm. She found them when she came in to open up this morning," said Roger as they walked through the hall. "She's waiting with the EMTs back in the Entertainment Center."

"The Entertainment Center?" asked Lew.

"That's what she calls it."

The hallway opened to a spacious, windowless room filled with round tables surrounded by chairs and a scattering of sofas with coffee tables. In contrast to the sunshine flooding the hallway, this interior was gloomy.

Looking toward the front of the room, Lew saw a small stage that appeared to be under construction. Four people in EMT uniforms were standing in front of a piano that seemed to be hovering in midair.

Even in the dim light she could make out a series of wire ropes and pulleys that disappeared into a hole in the stage floor. To her left was an antique oak bar with a dozen padded stools. The wall behind the bar was lined with shelves holding bottles of liquor. The wall to the far right was covered floor to ceiling with dark green curtains. As Lew scanned the room she realized the proportions of the space were familiar.

She turned to Roger and whispered as they walked across the room toward the group at the far end, "Hey, I think I know this building. Isn't this the old Long Lake Supper Club? I'm sure it is. Behind those curtains is a wall of windows opening to a nice view of Long Lake. Too bad they're covered up.

"My grandparents used to come here years ago," said Lew. "They brought me here for dinner when I graduated from eighth grade. I remember they had a magician from Chicago performing that night. And when I was in high school, they used to have rock concerts here. After that, the place was sold and it's been closed for years."

"I wouldn't know," said Roger, who had grown up in Milwaukee and didn't arrive in the Northwoods until after marrying a local girl in his late twenties. "But it sure ain't magicians they got performing here these days." He raised his eyebrows as he spoke. "Nope, no magicians for sure."

"Any way we can get more light in here? Can we pull back those curtains?" asked Lew, glancing overhead. "Hard to see . . . Joe? Are you able to see anything?" Lew had spotted Joe Teske, the lead paramedic on the team.

"I tried the curtains, Chief," said Roger, "but they're nailed shut, right to the studs in the wall. Want me to rip them open?"

"I'm doing okay," said Teske, walking over toward her. "I didn't want to risk moving or touching anything until you got here, Chief Ferris. Except that piano. I made the janitor show me how to lower it far enough so I could be sure we didn't have a victim in need of resuscitation or emergency transport." He held up both hands to show Lew they were gloved. "No fingerprints, Chief."

"Good," said Lew. "Fatalities?"

"'Fraid so. I'll leave it up to the pathologist for an expert call but it looks to me like both parties have been dead a few hours or more. Asphyxiated is my guess—crushed against the ceiling up there."

"That's strange. I wonder how the hell that happened," said Lew, staring at the grim scenario on the piano.

"Well," said Teske, "you got one of two scenarios: either a double murder or an expensive situation for the insurance company."

"Man, it is hard to see," said Lew, twisting around. "Is it possible to get more light in here?"

"Sure," said a husky voice from behind the bar. Rows of fluorescent lights flicked on overhead. "How's this?"

The explosion of light caught Lew off-guard. "That more than does it, thank you."

"It's the lighting I use when I'm cleaning—shows all the dirt, don't it?" The voice belonged to a thickset woman in cutoff jeans and a black sweatshirt. She remained standing in the shadows behind the bar as though reluctant to be seen.

After a quick glance back toward the stage where the ropes and pulleys suspending the piano in midair had come into better view, Lew turned to the paramedic and his team. "Sorry, Joe, but I don't think we can do more until the coroner gets here."

Teske nodded. "We know the drill. If you don't mind, we'll wait outside. Let me know when you need us." Raising his eyebrows, he said, "Haven't seen anything like this before."

After waving the EMTs off, Lew walked over to the woman who had just spoken. She had blowsy dark hair, which she wore very short and shoved behind her ears. The squareness of her facial features emphasized cheeks as loose as a squirrel's and wrinkled from years of smoking. Though Lew had a hard time guessing her age, she seemed vaguely familiar.

"Chief, this is Joyce Harmon," said Roger, pulling his shoulders back and speaking with as much authority as he was capable of. "She's the one I told you found the bodies. Joyce here is the, um, well, um, the *assistant* maintenance engineer for Buddy's Place. And, Joyce, this here is Chief Ferris—"

"I know who she is," said Joyce, her tone blunt. "Lew Ferris, right? Seen you at parent-teacher meetings years ago. Back when you were still working at the mill. Our daughters were in grade school together. And I'm the *janitor*, Officer Adamczak, not no engineer. Thought I told you that." She spoke with the sullenness of a person who doesn't expect to be listened to.

"Sorry," said Roger staring at the floor. "Just wanted to be sure I had your official title is all . . ." His voice trailed off in embarrassment.

Poor Roger. Lew knew he regretted his decision years earlier to give up his struggling insurance business in favor of what he thought would be an easy road to retirement: join the Loon Lake Police Department as one of two full-time police officers destined to empty parking meters until the day his pension check would appear.

But no sooner had Roger joined the department when the Loon Lake Town Council voted to remove the meters and hire Lewellyn Ferris fresh out of law enforcement training.

Once she was promoted to chief, Roger's life changed. He found himself in the uncomfortable position of having to arrest former insurance clients for DUIs, domestic disturbances, and outdated vehicle registrations. In short order he found himself banned from the Saturday afternoon poker games. The final blow was no more invites to fish walleye in Canada.

In spite of those disappointments, Roger tried his best. But his demeanor was so mild that few miscreants believed him when he identified himself as being a police officer—even when he was in uniform. Then there was his chronic stomach ailment, which occurred like clockwork whenever he drew a holiday weekend assignment.

And so it was that Loon Lake Police Chief Lewellyn Ferris couldn't help but count the days to Officer Adamczak's retirement.

"Fred Smith is the maintenance engineer and I'm just the janitor," Joyce said. "I pick up the slack here and over at Deer Creek. Mainly I pick up trash." She gave a halfhearted grin.

"The private preserve next door?" Lew's question was rhetorical.

"Yep. Been working there fourteen years."

"That doesn't sound like a bad job. I'll bet they pay you pretty well. Deer Creek is quite the place, I hear." Even as she spoke Lew knew that was an understatement.

Every adult and teenager in Loon Lake was well aware of the Deer Creek Fishing and Hunting Preserve—referred to by locals as Deer Creek. Private land with three private lakes stocked with some of the Northwoods' largest walleye and bass, Deer Creek is off-limits to locals, including employees.

During the peak seasons of summer and fall, when half a dozen residents from the area might be working there, they were given lodging in a barracks with single bedrooms, shared baths. Preserve rules dictated that nonmembers, i.e. employees, had no access to the lakes or forest trails. They had to enter and leave on specified "utility" roads and even then at certain hours.

Only Deer Creek members are allowed to enter and leave via the main drive as well as the lanes winding through the stunning forests of cedar, hemlock, and ancient white pine. And those members are three, sometimes four, generations removed from the half-dozen men—lumber barons and railroad titans from Chicago—who founded the private club in the late 1800s.

Even today, only people related by blood to the "founding fathers" are ever admitted to membership, which means there can never be more than 200 families able to enjoy one of the last remaining reserves of virgin timber in Wisconsin: over a thousand acres where never a living tree has been cut down.

But what may be true of its trees was not true of the Deer Creek member who lay face-down on top of the white baby grand piano hovering three feet over the stage at the far end of the Entertainment Center in Buddy's Place. Face-down on top of an individual who was most certainly *not* a member of the Deer Creek Fishing and Hunting Preserve.

Chapter Four

"Mrs. Harmon, do you know who those people are?" asked Lew, staring at the top of the piano where the fluorescent lighting illuminated the two bodies, better defining how one was pinned on top of the other and clarifying that the foot hanging over one edge of the piano belonged to a man. A naked man.

Under his head, which was turned toward the back wall, was a spray of blonde spiked hair. The hair belonged to a smaller body, also naked but barely visible beneath the other.

"*Ms.*, please, Chief Ferris," said Joyce. "I'm not Mrs.—I'm Ms. I been divorced twenty years thank the Lord. But can you just call me Joyce?"

"Certainly. So, *Joyce*," said Lew, determined to be patient, "do you know the victims?"

"Yes, I do." The answer was loud and firm. "That there man on top is Chet Wright, he owns this place. Bought it 'bout eighteen months ago and shipped that piano up from New Orleans. The woman is Tiffany Niedermeier. He's from Rhinelander. I don't know where the hell she's from."

And from the sound of it you don't much care, thought Lew. "Do you know anyone who will?"

"Will what?"

"Will know where the female victim is from—where she lives. We'll have to reach her next of kin."

"Oh, jeez, how the hell would I know? Ask the woman who works with her. She'll be here soon enough."

"All right," said Lew, pulling on a pair of nitrile gloves. "I'll deal with that later. Right now, I'd like to see if we can lower that piano all the way to the stage. And, Roger," she said looking over at the officer standing nearby, "do you have nitrile gloves on? Until I know if this is an accident or not, I want nothing touched. That includes you, Joyce."

Joyce had started to move forward but Lew put out a hand to stop her. "Officer Adamczak told you where to walk so we don't contaminate the area. Correct?"

The woman nodded. "He did. I know I'm s'posed to walk right where the two of you are walking."

Satisfied with her answer, Lew paused to study the scene overhead. "Right now what I'd like to know is . . ." Lew left her words hanging.

"How that piano ended way up on the ceiling?" Joyce finished the question for her. "I have no idea." She glanced over at Roger. "He already asked me that. I haven't a clue."

Lew turned to give the woman a long look: now she was sure where she had seen her before. "Say, Joyce, aren't you one of the Freundlichs?" She knew she was deliberately changing the subject but she had a hunch that Joyce knew more than she was saying. She also knew that getting the woman to open up was going to be a challenge.

"Yep, I'll bet you knew my brothers, hey?"

Yes, Lew did. "Butch was in my class but he dropped out of school before graduating, didn't he?"

"That's right. My little sister, Debbie, and I are the only ones who graduated."

Joyce was one of two girls in a family of five. Her brothers—known to everyone as "those Freddie boys"—had spent their teens in and out of the Loon Lake jail too many times to count. Their misdemeanors ranged from vandalism in the schoolyard to petty theft and illegal exhaust pipes on their motorcycles, which they liked to ride, roaring, through a sleeping Loon Lake hours before dawn.

Lew recalled, too, that Joyce's former husband had hung out with the Freddie boys and was rumored to have beaten her up. He might be long gone but the chip on Joyce's shoulder appeared to be permanent. However, there was one Freundlich male who did not have a police record.

"Your dad ran the TV repair shop at the corner of Pine and Brown, right?" Lew asked. She looked over to the hallway as she spoke, hoping to see Pecore walk in, but no sign of him yet.

"Yep. Those days he owned the building, too."

"My grandfather used to say he was the smartest electrician he ever ran into."

"Really?" Joyce's voice softened.

"And didn't you work in his shop? I remember helping my grandpa carry in one of those old TV consoles for repair and I'm pretty sure I saw you there. I mean, we were both kids back then, but am I right?"

"Man, that was a l-o-o-n-g time ago," said Joyce. "No one even repairs a TV anymore. And do you know how hard it is to find a good electrician these days? But, yep, you're right. My dad taught me how to be an electrician. I'm darn good, too. That's a lot of what I do here and over at Deer Creek."

"In addition to picking up trash?" Lew grinned.

"Yeah," Joyce chuckled. "You got me on that.

"Y'know, it is so funny how my brothers were never interested in Dad's business but I love the stuff. Hell, I've been working with

Chet to put in lighted stripper poles over there." She motioned toward the side of the stage. "Be a lot more interesting than some girl twisting herself around a plain old pole. The ones I ordered have these cool LED lights running up and down—" She stopped. "Guess that won't be happening, will it."

Lew shrugged. "Hard to say. Once we know what happened—could be someone will buy this place and want to keep it open . . ." As a hopeful expression spread across Joyce's face, Lew decided to press for more.

"Joyce, it's obvious you're the expert around here. Would you mind walking me through what you think *might* have happened? The EMTs and I can't do much more until the coroner gets here anyway. Depending on what you can tell me, I may have to call in the Wausau boys, too."

"The Wausau boys?" asked Joyce, walking over to stand near Lew. Her voice was lighter now, less guarded. "Who are they?"

"The Wausau Crime Lab. Often when there's been a certain type of felony crime committed, we pay them to process the crime scene. Especially if there's been a homicide or attempted murder. Loon Lake doesn't have the budget for the equipment much less the forensic expertise needed. I'm lucky to have computers."

Lew dropped her voice as if sharing a secret. "I mean, the coroner I'm waiting for used to run a bar, for God's sake. The only thing he's good for is telling me if someone is alive or dead."

With that comment and with the hope that Joyce wasn't a close relative of Pecore, Lew checked her watch. "Jeez Louise, Roger, where on earth *is* Pecore? I called him a good fifteen minutes ago—he should be here by now. If he hasn't arrived in five minutes, would you please call dispatch and ask Marlaine to check on him? This is unacceptable."

Chapter Five

"This was all Chet's idea," said Joyce with a wave at the ropes and pulleys while Roger stepped away to call dispatch. "He told me he'd seen a dancer perform on a piano years ago and he thought it was so cool. He said she was all dressed in these big feathers and stood perfectly still on the piano as it came down from above. At first he thought she was a statue.

"But when the piano reached the stage, music started and the dancer started to strip. One feather at a time and all while dancing on the piano. When she had taken everything off, she posed like the statue again and the piano carried her up, up and away." Joyce raised her hands, palms up, to demonstrate.

"Chet said she was so gorgeous—she was like an angel. So that's what he wanted Tiffany to do, but we had a problem. Tiffany looked sexy, like with her top off and stuff, at least Chet thought so—she was too bony to be sexy if you ask me—but she was a terrible dancer. She'd been dancing here for at least three months, six nights a week and who knows how many times a night, yet every time the piano would start to go up, she'd stumble and almost fall off.

"I have to say that twice she did fall but not far enough to hurt herself. She tried to say it was my fault—that the darn thing jerked when it started up—but that's a lie. I keep it well oiled. The piano works fine. It's the dancer."

Lew couldn't resist asking, "Did this Tiffany wear feathers?"

A hint of humor flashed at the back of Joyce's eyes. "No, Tiffany did not wear feathers. She should have. Anything, even feathers would have been better than what she wore. And, believe you me," Joyce rolled her eyes, "Tiffany Niedermeier is no angel.

"Tell you the truth, I think she's a pretty awful person . . . *was* a pretty awful person. And I've known 'awful,' doncha know."

Joyce opened her mouth ready to add further insult to the memory of the individual pinned on the piano but Lew jumped in before she could say more. "Okay, we can talk about that later. Right now I'd like you to show me how the piano and the lift system works. I am trying to understand what has happened here."

"Oh sure," said Joyce, "sorry if I got carried away talking about Tiffany. See up there? Can you see where there's a balcony over to one side?"

"Yes," said Lew, "I see it."

"Well, there is a stairway behind the stage that leads to the balcony and that's where the dancer waits before stepping onto the piano."

"And who plays the piano?" asked Lew. "Chet?"

"Gosh no. That's a player piano. Now come over this way and I'll show you how this whole shebang operates."

Lew followed Joyce over to the wall just to the right of the stage where there was an electric utility box with two levers inside. The box was hidden behind a short curtain so audience members wouldn't get a good look.

"This here sends the piano up," said Joyce. She started to reach for the lever but Lew grabbed her arm.

"No, please don't touch that. We need to check for fingerprints."

"Oh, sure, sorry I keep forgetting," said Joyce, backing up a step. "That lever to the left brings the piano down. Up above there are two levers just like these on the wall next to the balcony."

"So the piano can be operated from either direction, up or down?"

"Correct," said Joyce. "Chet got all this equipment from a bar in New Orleans that was being demolished. It is *not* state of the art. I wanted to update the wiring so you could adjust the speed of the piano's rising and lowering just like you do a dimmer on a light switch.

"I also wanted to install a safety that could be triggered by movement like a deer cam, y'know—but Chet didn't want to spend the money. What I *was* able to do was install the box up there in such a way that the levers could be easily reached when you are standing on the piano, but you do have to reach for them."

"Are you saying that there was no safety to stop the piano from going up too high?"

"That's right. It didn't need one coming down because it was built to stop when it reached the stage. Going up we assumed everyone would know to stop it when they could reach the levers."

"Does everyone working here know how this works?"

"Well, I do, my boss the head maintenance guy does, Chet, of course, and Nina and Tiffany. Tiffany is the only one allowed to dance on the piano. Actually she's the only one who agreed to 'cause she got paid more. Nina dances part-time. Mostly she hosts."

"Hosts?"

"You know, encourages patrons to stay late, order more drinks. That kind of stuff. Nina or Chet will be the one to push the lever to raise the piano when Tiffany gives the signal. Once the piano reached the balcony, Tiffany would pull the lever to stop it.

"Sometimes she would climb off then let the piano go all the way up to the ceiling. That's where it was stored after the show and that's how high it was when I got here this morning."

"I see . . ." Lew hesitated before asking, "Joyce, if two people were on the piano would it take a third person to push the lever that moved that piano up so high?"

"Not sure. I mean, someone might have kicked it with their foot by accident."

Roger, who had been standing nearby and listening said, "What if when they were climbing on? Could they have hit the lever then?"

"Maybe." Joyce shrugged. "I will say that no one has ever had the damn thing move by accident—if that helps. Although . . ."

"Although what?" asked Lew.

"This box here," Joyce pointed to the utility box in front of them, "has an emergency switch that allows these levers to overrule the ones upstairs. I forgot about that."

After a moment of thought, Lew said, "If we shift a lever now will the piano come down to the stage level and stop?"

"It should. Are you ready for me to bring it down?"

"One more question before you do that. Why on earth would those two people have been on top of the piano? I mean, I know what they were doing—but why *there*?"

"It was this weird idea Chet had," said Joyce. "He found it exciting, I guess. Tiffany didn't help. She kind of lured him along. I know 'cause a couple times I was working late and found the two of them fooling around in here after hours. And, boy, when Chet's wife found out about the piano and Tiffany: that was the end of that marriage."

"So Chet Wright is divorced?"

"Not quite."

Lew's cell phone rang. "It's dispatch, excuse me. Yes, Marlaine?"

"Chief, Mr. Pecore hit a deer on his way out there. I just had a call from the county sheriff. They've got the Oneida County Rescue Squad on its way to pry him from the car and get him to the hospital in Rhinelander."

"*Pry him from the car?*" Lew was stupefied.

"They told me the deer went through the windshield. The car is totaled and Mr. Pecore's cut pretty bad. He may have a broken collarbone . . ."

Chapter Six

"How do those waders feel? Are they too long?" asked Osborne as eleven-year-old Mason, tugging at an elastic belt around her waist, pushed through the curtain in front of the women's dressing room at Ralph's Sporting Goods. She paused to look at herself in the long dressing room mirror.

Seated nearby on a folding chair, her grandfather studied the fit of the waders, which were a women's size small. After trying on three pairs—the price tags increasing exponentially with each—these looked the most comfortable.

"I like these best, Grandpa," said Mason, arms extended as she twirled in front of the dressing room mirrors.

Her twirl reminded Osborne of watching Lew in the trout stream: from her toes to her fingertips, every cast from her fly rod was as elegant as a great blue heron taking wing. It also reminded him that more than a week had passed since he and Lew had last fly-fished together.

That had to change. August with its too-warm waters would be here too soon. He made a mental note to demand yet another lesson on the technique he was finding impossible: shooting line. Why his timing was so off—

"These waders aren't stiff like those others," said Mason, interrupting his thoughts.

Osborne reached over to check the price tag: just short of $300. And that was before adding the boots. The good news was that Mason's shoe size was the same as a women's small in lightweight wading boots, so Ralph should be able to outfit her. The morning was turning into a more expensive shopping expedition than he had anticipated.

It didn't help that he had hoped to persuade Lew to come along if only for a few minutes to get her expert opinion on the best fishing gear for a woman, especially a young girl. More than once she had mentioned that she had started fishing under the guidance of her grandfather when she was just a kid Mason's age. But the emergency call from Roger Adamczak had made that impossible.

And there was no putting it off. Mason was too excited over her summer job helping his neighbor, Ray Pradt, as he coached the Wisconsin State College fishing team to ask her to wait another minute before getting outfitted.

"Our first meeting with the team is this afternoon, Gramps," she had said when she announced the news of her hiring earlier that morning. "Ray said they'll be strategizing. I have to look like I know what I'm doing, you know."

When he heard that, Osborne had struggled to suppress a smile. It wasn't like Mason had much of a clue as to what the "team" would be doing. Her job was to be the "gofer" for the two boys on the team.

Working from shore, she would be responsible for keeping their tackle organized before and after they fished, and making sure the cooler was packed with ice, sodas, cheese curds, and peanut butter sandwiches. Ray also wanted her to have waders on hand in order to keep the shallow area around his dock free of floating logs, dead fish, or debris from the speedboats and pontoons crowding the lake—all serious responsibilities for an eleven-year-old girl who would be paid $10 a day to help out.

Ten dollars that would not go far paying for top-of-the-line waders. The only good news was she already owned a swimsuit, T-shirts, shorts, sun hats, and water shoes. Those items plus a rain jacket *and* the waders should have her ready for action.

Osborne maintained a serious expression as he checked out the fit of the most expensive waders in the shop. He didn't mind buying them for Mason. He knew she was beyond thrilled to have been hired: "*Me*—not that stupid Tim Rasmusson, Gramps."

Her new boss was not only Osborne's neighbor but one of the Northwoods' most respected fishing guides. Mason herself was hardly new to the sport, as Osborne had made sure to have each of his three grandchildren fishing before they turned four. But it was Mason and her younger brother, Cody, who most loved being on water.

And it wasn't just that his granddaughter loved to fish and that being around the team would teach her a lot about muskie fishing, but it was how being paid to help out would make her feel: smart, capable, a team player. Not a bad feeling for a young girl to have.

And who knows, thought Osborne. She might grow up and become CEO of Ranger Boats someday, making the purchase of new waders a small price to pay.

But he had another reason for indulging Mason. She was the grandchild who had inherited the genetic markers of Osborne's Métis ancestors. Like him, she had olive skin that tanned dark under the summer sun, high cheekbones, and hair black as lake water on a frigid day.

Add to that she was the middle child in his daughter Erin's family, sandwiched between the eldest girl and the first boy. She was the quiet one, the reader. While he wouldn't say she was his favorite (because he didn't believe in picking favorites), Mason had a special place in her grandfather's heart.

Osborne knew that Ray was aware he had made a wise choice. He couldn't have found a more enthusiastic helper. Mason loved being outdoors and she was so full of energy she drove her parents nuts. So while their daughter was ecstatic over her new job, Erin and Mark were thrilled she would have Ray and the college boys to keep her busy. At least for the next three days.

"Say, Doc," said Ralph, owner of the sporting-goods store, as he walked up holding two pairs of wading boots, "have her try these with those waders. One pair should work."

Before Osborne could check the price tag on the boots, his cell phone trilled its ringtone medley of birdsongs. "Lew? You back already?"

"Doc, I need you—"

Before she could finish, he jumped in to say, "Under most circumstances those words would make me happy but I'm tied up helping Mason buy waders right now. Would you believe she has a job working for—"

Lew interrupted before he could finish, her voice tense. "Doc, Pecore hit a deer on his way out here. They're taking him to the emergency room. Meantime I'm looking at two people definitely deceased and under very peculiar circumstances. I'm not sure if this is an accident or worse.

"I am so sorry to ruin your morning but I need you out at the old Long Lake Supper Club ASAP. They call it Buddy's Place now. You know where I mean? Right next door to Deer Creek? Sorry, but you are my only option and I'm worried about keeping the EMTs waiting. They've already had two other emergency calls and had to send ambulances from Three Lakes and Eagle River."

"Not to worry, I'll manage," said Osborne, watching as Mason pulled the first wading boot on. "I'll leave right now—have to run home for my black bag and drop the dog off. That should take less than ten minutes. Then I'll be heading your way."

He could hear Lew exhale in relief. "Thank you. I'm calling the Wausau boys right now. Just so you know we may be here awhile. I . . . it's strictly a gut feeling but I doubt this is an accident, Doc.

"Oh, shoot, one more thing. Can you call Ray and let him know the situation? If he can follow you out here with his camera gear, I need photos. Now that I think of it maybe it's a blessing that Pecore can't make it—Ray takes better photos. But tell him to be sure to bring extra lighting. He may need it."

"Got it."

Tucking his phone away, Osborne looked over at his granddaughter. "Mason, Chief Ferris has an emergency and needs my help. I know you can handle everything here. We can talk about sharing the cost of these waders and boots later. Right now I'm going to give Ralph my credit card. He'll wrap everything up for you. Can you get home okay?"

Mason frowned at him. "Grandpa, I live two blocks away. Of course I can get home by myself." She smiled. "This is very cool stuff and I'm going to bring it all to the meeting with Ray and the team.

"Oh, right, Mom asked me to see if you could pick me up and give me a ride to Ray's for the meeting? And I might have to stay overnight with you. She said she'd give you a call later. Is that okay, Grandpa?"

"What time is this meeting at Ray's?"

"Five o'clock."

"Sure, honey. I'll pick you up at four thirty."

"Oh, thanks, Grandpa." Mason got to her feet, gave a little hop and hugged Osborne, who ruffled her hair. She paused and looked up at him, concern in her eyes. "Do you think I have to start calling Ray Mr. Pradt?"

"You ask him, kiddo," said Osborne. "Maybe. Won't *that* be weird?"

As he headed out the front door of Ralph's Sporting Goods, Osborne couldn't resist thinking: Five hundred dollars well spent, and now on to help the smartest woman I know. Life is not bad.

Chapter Seven

A sense of dread low in her gut, Lew punched in the number for the director of the Wausau Crime Lab. Listening as the phone rang, she reminded herself to stay civil but firm. And sure enough the phone was answered by one of the few people in the universe whom she despised.

"Jesperson here. That you, Looney Tunes?" (Stay civil, Lewellyn. Do not take the bait.)

"Morning, Doug. I imagine you're working the holiday shift as usual?"

It was her way of letting him know that she knew he was double-dipping. Perfectly legal but not appreciated by Lew and a few others in law enforcement who had been relieved to hear of his retirement only to discover he had worked a scheme to get full retirement benefits plus holiday pay by offering to sub for the regular staff when they took time off.

"Oh yeah. One more day to go and I'm off for three months. Wife and I are taking an Alaskan cruise. So what's worrying your pretty little head? Someone rob Pat's Bar?" Strictly for the benefit of her own mental health, Lew rolled her eyes and, for a split second, held the phone away from her ear.

"Thank you, Doug. I wish that's all it was and you know we can handle anything like that. No, I have two victims of an industrial accident or possibly worse . . ."

After quickly sketching out the scene at Buddy's Place, Lew was dismayed to hear excitement in Doug's voice. She had hoped he would assign the case to one of his forensic techs and not bother with it himself.

Lewellyn Ferris found Doug Jesperson to be—in spite of his lofty position as the retired director of the Wausau Crime Lab—a creep. *A genuine four-star creep.* Not only did he patronize her but he had a nasty habit of slipping dirty jokes into their professional discussions.

Every single time she met with the guy she found herself having to say, "Doug, you know I am not interested in that kind of humor." More than once she'd had to physically walk away before he got the message. But while she could walk away from the jokes, she could not avoid his repeated diatribes that he did not think "girls belong in law enforcement. They just don't have the authoritative presence, you know?"

No, she didn't know, and she refused to discuss it.

But the worst was when he would stand just a little too close, invading her personal space. Yet he never crossed the line. He had enough sense to know that could be a big mistake.

The everyday fact of life in the Northwoods was that the tiny Loon Lake Police Department with its three officers and one drunken coroner had to depend on the Wausau Crime Lab when major crimes such as homicides needed investigating. Fortunately for Lew, not all the "Wausau boys" were like Doug Jesperson.

At the moment, however, the hours ahead were not looking good: Doug was sounding w-a-a-y too interested in the scene at Buddy's Place.

"Hey, are you kidding me?" Lew heard him say. "What you have just described sounds like one juicy scenario. This could get me a speaking gig down at the university during their next national conference on sex crimes. Give me an hour, Miss Chief. I'll copter up and bring one of our docs along. Hold on while I see who's in the office."

Lew's spirits sagged. On top of everything else was she now going to have to deal with Jesperson's idiocy? Some days life was not fair.

"Oops." Doug was back on the line. "My secretary just reminded me that my wife wants me home by noon. We got a dinner flight to Seattle."

"That's too bad," said Lew. "Any chance Bruce Peters might step in?"

"Doubt it. He's off at a workshop on body cameras in Appleton—but let me check." Again he put her on hold. He was back in less than a minute. "Lucky you, Looney Tunes, they just finished up. He said he's available but wants the details from you, so I'm patching you through."

"Chief Ferris?" Now this was a voice she liked to hear. "What are the water temps up there? Still cool enough for a little stream fishing? I just bought a new fly rod—a three-weight—and could use some coaching. My roll cast is real sloppy."

"Sounds like you might have the wrong line or your leader is too heavy. Sure, Bruce, we can work something out. But first let me tell you what I'm looking at up here . . ."

When she had finished describing the scene at Buddy's Place, Bruce gave a low whistle.

"Whoa. Any chance those victims could have been killed elsewhere and the bodies arranged the way you're describing? I mean, why would two people climb on top of a piano? Sounds like deviant involvement to me."

"I hadn't thought of that," said Lew. "Afraid I have to leave that to you and your people to figure out."

"And we will," said Bruce with the same determination he used when struggling to cast into the wind while stumbling over rocks in the trout stream. "We'll figure it out. I'll send up our van and alert pathology to make room for two body bags. We'll do the autopsies down here.

"Give me an hour and a half, Chief. I'm almost to Wausau, then I have to grab an overnight bag and sign off on these arrangements."

"Good," said Lew. "I'll get you reservations at the Loon Lake Motel. Two nights okay? Give us time for fishing tomorrow evening?"

"You betcha."

"Oh, one more question, Bruce. I mentioned this piano is still up overhead, but there is a lever that will bring it down. One of the paramedics here lowered it enough to be sure no one was alive—"

"Oh, oh. Don't like hearing that. Did he wear gloves?"

"Yes, of course. Joe knows the protocol. If we wear nitrile gloves, is it okay to lower it further so my acting coroner—you know Doc Osborne—can start work on the death certificates? It's impossible to get a close view of the victims otherwise."

"Please do not do that, Chief. He won't be able to complete the certificates until I can confirm cause of death anyway. And who knows yet if you have an accident or a double homicide. Better to not touch a thing in case there are prints or any other evidence close by. And, hey, say hi to Doc for me. Your man Pecore overserved again?"

"It's a long story, Bruce. I'll fill you in when you get here." Relieved, Lew hung up.

Walking over to the waiting ambulance crew, she motioned to Joe Teske, who hurried over. "It's okay, Joe, you and your crew can go back to town," she said. "I've got Bruce Peters from the Wausau Crime Lab on his way up. Their van will run the victims down to Wausau for autopsies."

Before she could walk back across the room to let Roger know what was happening, the silhouette of a man appeared in the hallway at the entrance to the Entertainment Center. "Holy hell, what is *this*?" he cried, racing through the room toward the stage.

"Joyce, goddammit, why didn't you call me!" he shouted at Joyce, who was sitting in the chair where Lew had instructed her to wait. Joyce's face froze as he approached. She rose from her chair.

"Stop right there, sir," said Lew, stepping forward to block his way. "Do *not* take another step. Stay right where you are. That yellow tape outside means you should not have entered the building. This may be a crime scene. Now back up."

"But I'm in charge here—"

"Not now, you aren't."

Lew continued to move toward him, forcing him back. "Way back—into the hallway." The man, dressed in dark green work clothes, looked undecided until the authority in Lew's voice and a good look at her khaki police uniform convinced him to do what she said.

"Good. Now, what is your name, why are you here, and will you please stop shouting," said Lew as she pulled a notepad from her back pocket.

"He's Fred Smith, my boss," said Joyce who, along with Roger, had followed Lew out to the hallway. "Fred, I tried to call you right after I called nine-one-one but all I got was voice mail and right then this officer," she said, pointing at Roger, "came running in and I forgot to leave a message."

"*You forgot to leave a message?*" The man's voice thundered through the hall. "What the hell time was this anyway? You were late again, weren't you? That's why you didn't call. What did I tell you last week? One more time showing up late and you are out of here. I am sick and tired of—"

"No, I was here early. I can show you—"

"Excuse me, mister. I can tell you what time she called. It was two minutes after nine that dispatch called me," said Roger, holding up his cell phone.

The man named Fred had pulled out a cell phone of his own, ready to challenge the timing, only to pause.

"Is your phone off?" asked Lew.

"No, but I had an HVAC issue next door at Deer Creek," said Fred in a smaller voice. "I must have set it by my toolkit and didn't hear the ring. You're right, Joyce, I see your call now."

"Enough of this," said Lew. "I have my deputy coroner and a forensic team from the Wausau Crime Lab arriving shortly. So, Fred Smith, is it? Middle initial?"

"Yes, T for Thomas," said Smith. He was of medium height with light brown hair in a buzz cut and a mild face, the kind of face you don't remember. "I'm the maintenance engineer for the Deer Creek Fishing and Hunting Preserve and for this place."

"All right, Mr. Smith, the first information I need from you is whom do you suggest I contact to get next of kin information on the victims?" asked Lew. "Joyce has identified them as Tiffany Niedermeier, an employee of Buddy's Place, and the owner, Chet Wright. I'm going to assume you're familiar with both?"

"Is it okay if I sit down?" asked Fred, his voice shaking. Lew nodded. He took a few steps into the Entertainment Center, reached off to the side for a chair, sat down heavily, took a deep breath, and asked, "You're not serious? That's who . . ." His voice trailed off.

"Oh, come on, Fred," said Joyce. "Who the hell else hangs out here after hours. You know that."

Lew could not miss the disgust in Joyce's voice: sign of a healthy working relationship. No doubt the woman kept her job only because she was willing to do garbage pickup.

Fred straightened up. "Joyce is right. Tiffany is one to be drinking here after hours." He turned toward Lew. "She says she needs to wind down after her performance. I don't know how late she stays though. My shift is up at nine. Nine in the evening that is. Joyce, here, comes in at nine in the morning to clean up."

"But what about Chet Wright. Why would he be here?"

Joyce snorted.

From the corner of her eye, Lew saw Osborne coming down the hall. As he got near she called to him, "Doc, you're just in time. Let me move everyone out of here so you can work. Roger? Will you please escort Joyce and Mr. Smith out to the front hall? Don't either of you leave until I get back to you, but if you can call someone with information on next of kin that will be very helpful."

"I've got a phone number for Mrs. Wright," said Fred, jumping to his feet. "I know the Wright family real well. They're members of Deer Creek and—"

Before he could say more, Lew asked, "Does this club belong to Deer Creek?"

"Um . . . I don't know . . . maybe sort of," said Fred, stammering. "Maybe? I'm not sure though. You better ask Mrs. Wright."

"Okay, forget I asked," said Lew with a sense she was getting nowhere talking to the guy. "Just get me the number, please," she said as she walked away to catch up with Osborne.

Chapter Eight

After pulling on nitrile gloves and paper slippers, Osborne climbed the narrow stairway to the upper platform, which put him in a position to look down at the piano and its macabre burden. Steadying himself against a flimsy railing that extended only half the width of the platform he leaned down and forward to study Chet Wright's face.

The eyes were open and bloodshot. Ah, thought Osborne, why was he not surprised that Wright was intoxicated when he died? Or under the influence of drugs, in which Chet was known to indulge?

Of course, he could be wrong but having known Chet Wright since he was a boy growing up in Loon Lake, Osborne had good reason to make the assumption. For the moment, he would keep that thought to himself. Whatever the official reason for the bloodshot eyes would be for the pathologist to decide. Osborne's decision was the easy one: the man was dead.

Nor was there any sign of life in the woman, whose face was turned away, her body still. One slender forearm was visible from beneath her partner's body. Taking care not to fall off the platform, Osborne reach down with one hand to test for a pulse. Not a flicker.

Given that Chet was not a small man, Osborne guessed the combination of his bulk plus pressure from the apparatus pushing the piano up against the ceiling likely crushed her to death. But all that he could officially note in his capacity as deputy coroner was the fact that the woman who appeared to be Tiffany Niedermeier was no longer alive. Even then he could not officially record the names of either victim until members of their respective families had identified them. That meant that for the moment his job was done.

Osborne stood upright, stretching, before backing his way down the stairs that led up to the platform. As he felt for each step, he shook his head in quiet amazement. How on earth had he—a widowed, retired dentist age sixty-three going on sixty-four, father of two and grandfather of three—found himself identifying dead bodies? Dead bodies on top of a piano in a strip joint no less?

Not that he minded ramping up his knowledge of dental forensics: he had always loved doing research in his field and dental charts were still the gold standard for identifying dead bodies. But along with this unplanned second career (part-time though it was) had come a warm if not intimate relationship with the law enforcement officer in charge of deputizing him. Getting to know Lewellyn Ferris had changed his world. When she was around something in him opened, something too long shut.

No sir. This was not what he had expected two and a half years ago when he signed up for lessons on how to cast the fly rod he had kept hidden from his late wife, who had considered fishing a waste of time that drained money from his dental practice—money better spent on a bigger house, new furniture, nice clothes, and dinner parties, all the amenities essential to her status in her bridge club. Osborne never knew when it was during the months he courted Mary Lee that he forgot to mention the entire reason he practiced dentistry: so he could afford to fish.

Ruminating on these unforeseen changes in his life, Osborne was halfway down the stairs when he glanced over to his right. He stopped midstair, mesmerized by what he saw.

In a small closet below the stairs and to the right of the stage, cordoned off so it wasn't visible to the audience, was a workbench that had been built under a blacked-out window. The bench held a white plastic pail containing what appeared to be cleaning supplies. Beside the pail and on the table in front of the window were two footprints. Osborne stared at the prints trying to understand why they would be on *top* of the workbench unless . . .

"Lew," he said, raising his voice so he could be heard out in the Entertainment Center, "I mean, Chief Ferris, you better see this, hurry."

"What is it, Doc?" Lew appeared at the base of the stairs. "Can it wait? I'm on the phone getting names and numbers of next of kin from the manager over at Deer Creek. When I mentioned the name of the woman, Tiffany Niedermeier, turns out she was waiting tables there up until recently so he's got her mother's name—"

"You have to see this," said Osborne, still perched on the stairs and pointing down. Raising one hand while she finished her phone conversation, Lew waited until she was off her cell phone before pulling back the canvas drop that hid the closet and walked over to the workbench. She studied the tabletop. She leaned down to give the prints a close look.

"Sand. Must be from right outside this window. Hold on while I get Roger on this. I want no one walking around this building until we know how these prints got here. Could be more tracks outside."

"I would barricade the entire area between here and the Deer Creek Fishing and Hunting Preserve as well as the woods along the west side and up to the road," said Osborne. "Could be nothing or there could be tracks indicating that someone broke in here recently. And why would they do that? Isn't this place open until after two in the morning?"

Nodding in agreement, Lew glanced at her watch. "How much longer till Ray gets here?" she asked. "I'll ask him to check for any sign of intruders, although I imagine Joyce and her boss Fred walk around this place a good deal." She peered through a scratch in the blackened window. "The trash bins are right outside."

"Ray is on his way but he's going to be short on time, Lew. He has a meeting with his tournament fishing team at five so he might not have time to do both the photos and the tracking. I know this because he's hired Mason to help him and I've promised to get her to that meeting."

With a look of exasperation, Lew said, "Are you kidding me? Man, what else can go wrong today? Jeez Louise."

After a moment's thought, she calmed down. "All right, good to know. If Bruce doesn't take forever getting here, I should be able to have him or his colleague take the photos while Ray works the outside. Bruce prefers it that way anyhow."

A vibration from the walkie-talkie on Lew's belt caused her to grab the unit and give it a quick glance. "It's Roger. He needs me—and I need him."

As Lew headed off, Osborne finished letting himself down the stairs. Then, taking care not to touch anything and to stand in exactly the same space where Lew had stood moments earlier, he took a closer look at the impressions on the workbench. The footprints were outlined in sand and so well defined that, if he had to guess, the individual perched there had been wearing either a hiking boot or a running shoe—footwear with a defined pattern on the sole.

"Dr. Osborne, can you come out here, please?" called Lew from the main room and speaking so formally he knew someone other than Ray or Bruce must have arrived.

Walking back into the Entertainment Center, Osborne found her standing with two people, a man and a woman. He knew the woman. Chet's soon-to-be ex-wife but now his widow: Karen Wright. He did not recognize the man who stepped forward to introduce himself. "Ty Wallis, Dr. Osborne. I'm the manager for the Deer Creek Preserve. I was able to reach Mrs. Wright—" As he spoke he turned to the woman beside him.

"And I drove right over," said Karen. Looking up she asked, "Is that the accident Ty called about?"

"Yes," said Osborne, "we're in the process of confirming the other victim's identity but it is a woman. Karen, I'm so sorry about what's happened here." He looked over at Lew and said, "Karen is a former patient of mine. We've known one another for what—nearly thirty years?"

"Years ago, even before I was engaged to marry Chet," said Karen. "Yes, we go back a ways, don't we, Dr. Osborne?" A wisp of a smile crossed her face.

Again she looked up at the piano and its grim burden. "I have no idea what I'm looking at but I've been expecting something horrible to happen." She spoke in such a low voice both Lew and Osborne had to lean in close to be able to hear her better. Her expression struck Osborne as sad but relieved.

Lew's eyes widened. "Really? You knew about the woman and . . ."

"Woman? Try *women*. There have been many women," said Karen, her voice louder. "Chief Ferris, this is hardly the first time that my husband has been found with another woman. Chet and I have lived separate lives for a long time. He's been living in the guesthouse on our property for over a year now and I filed for divorce two months ago. Dr. Osborne would know that, I'm sure. News travels fast in Loon Lake."

She gave a grim smile. Looking at Osborne, she said, "Maybe Erin mentioned it to you? I know Dr. Osborne's daughter," said Karen at the questioning look on Lew's face. "I see her at the golf course.

"Given what I've learned Chet has been up to recently, I would not have been surprised if you had called to say he committed suicide. But *this*? This *accident*?"

Peering overhead again, she shook her head in resignation. "Honestly, I know I should be shocked and horrified, but all I can really say is once again Chet found the easy way out. I'll bet he was dead drunk and never knew what happened." She managed a grim, tight smile that looked more resentful than anything.

The room was silent for a long moment. "That may be," said Lew, "but I doubt the woman up there was planning to kill herself."

Karen looked more closely at the piano suspended over the stage. "Oh . . . no, you are right about that. I'm sure whoever she is had other things in mind. Too bad she didn't know Chet better. Would you agree, Dr. Osborne? You've known Chet."

Yes, he did. Osborne knew Chet Wright all too well.

Chapter Nine

Some people are born with a silver spoon. Not Chester H. Wright, Jr. He got solid gold. An angelic-looking child who grew into a strikingly handsome teenager with an engaging smile, Chet parlayed a talent at tennis into an academic "pass," surviving college as a star athlete while majoring in frat life.

Nor did it hurt that he stood to inherit a bank account that promised to keep him free of worry over the future, a future ensured by the past.

Chet's great-grandfather, Herman Chester Wright, migrated to northern Wisconsin from Germany in 1876. He and two of his brothers started out as loggers before building and running sawmills. Canny businessmen, they saw the potential in railroads and soon controlled logging and rail operations across the state.

Herman was also one of the half-dozen men who established the Deer Creek Fishing and Hunting Preserve for the exclusive use of their families and heirs. Even as they made their fortunes clear-cutting the northern forests of Wisconsin, they had an ironclad rule that not a single living tree, evergreen or hardwood, could be harvested from their own private Deer Creek land—and one never has.

To this day the Deer Creek Fishing and Hunting Preserve is unique in the Midwest for its stands of virgin timber and walleye-rich private water. And to this day the only access a nonmember can ever have is through employment.

Herman's son and only heir, Chester Herman, Sr., was Chet's grandfather and he transformed the family fortune into a conglomerate owning banks, telephone companies, pharmaceuticals, and printing plants. On his death, Chet's father, Herman, Jr., sold all the family assets with the exception of one large printing plant. When he was killed in an auto accident in Arizona where he had retired, his widow sold the printing plant. She lived two more years before dying of lung cancer, after which her son and only child inherited $60 million.

Chet was twenty-two years old at the time, fresh out of college and recently wed to the cutest girl in his Loon Lake High School graduating class: Karen Riesman.

A tiny woman with slim hips and breasts that had excited the boys in her class since seventh grade, Karen wore her straight hair in a shiny black cap that framed her moon-shaped face. She had eyes black as her hair that danced when she talked to boys.

Dimples in both cheeks guaranteed she would look permanently happy. In high school she was head cheerleader, voted Homecoming Queen, and shared the prom throne with her future husband. No one doubted that Karen and Chet were made for each other.

After their marriage, the young couple hired a Chicago architect familiar to Chet's late parents to build them a magnificent brick home on property Chet had inherited on the western shore of Loon Lake. A year after they moved into their new home with its matching guesthouse, their dock looked like a marina, with two pontoons (one for parties of twenty or more), half a dozen Jet Skis, a cabin cruiser, and a ski boat. Life was promising.

Three years into their marriage, Chet lost everything in the stock market: a spectacular miscalculation. But just when they thought they would have to sell their home, one of his great-uncles died, leaving behind stock in a Canadian mining company and no heirs. Chet inherited $32 million. An equally spectacular recovery. He was one of those people for whom luck never runs out.

Over the next ten years, he gave up tennis for blackjack and craps—pastimes made easy, as casinos were springing up across the region. Gambling didn't appeal to Karen. For her it was golf, bridge, and shopping in the cities. What she did lose interest in—following two miscarriages and the news that she could never have children—was conjugal relations.

"I mean, more than once a month? Good grief," she had confided to her bridge club during one of their gossip sessions. Osborne's late wife, Mary Lee, had been there and repeated Karen's comment as a way of letting Osborne know that she wasn't the only woman who felt that way.

Whether it was his wife's coolness or the warmth generated by the casino culture, Chet drifted into a social life that didn't include Karen. He became a regular patron of gentlemen's clubs, where he drank so heavily that it was not unusual for his wife to find him sleeping it off on the lakeside deck of their beautiful home.

Karen didn't seem to mind the other women so much as the damage Chet caused: drunk, he parked his car on her newly planted flowerbeds; drunk, he stumbled through the foyer, knocking over a Chinese vase worth thousands.

The rumor in recent months was that his addictions had extended beyond the casino, the booze, and the women: two regulars in Osborne's coffee crowd, which met weekday mornings at six around the table at McDonald's, had learned from their wives, who had heard from their hairdressers, that cocaine was Chet's new mistress.

Could be that was the final blow to the Wright marriage, which now appeared so strained that news of divorce proceedings caught no one by surprise. Nor did anyone in the coffee crowd disagree with Herb Anderson when he intoned over his third cup, "Had to happen. That fellow was given too much too soon. Makes a man susceptible to the underside of life, y'know." The caffeinated philosophers around the table nodded in agreement tempered with schadenfreude.

Chapter Ten

"Chief Ferris, is there anything I can help with?" asked Ty Wallis from where he was standing behind Karen Wright. A tall, thin middle-aged man, he was dressed in dark slacks and a white long-sleeved shirt: a uniform that passed for business attire in the Northwoods. Both hands thrust deep in his pockets, he cleared his throat so often Osborne was tempted to ask if he needed a glass of water.

"Over many, many years Wright family members have been significant benefactors to our Deer Creek Preserve so anything I—"

"Please, tell her the truth, Ty," interrupted Karen. "If you won't, I'll have to." She spoke with a quiet forcefulness that reminded Osborne how even as a teenager she had impressed him with her thoughtful, serious ways. Not unlike Chet Wright's mother, as a matter of fact.

"Are you sure?" Ty asked. A guttural clearing of the throat this time.

"Very sure. It's going to come out one way or another. You know that, Ty."

The man studied the floor for a long moment, then coughed and cleared before saying, "Okay . . . I expect I'll lose my job over this . . . but Karen is right."

Eyes closed, he clamped his lips tight together and stood silent as if deliberating where to start. Everyone waited. Finally he said, "I have been trying to broker—not sure if that's the right word—let's say 'reach an agreement' between Chet and three members of the preserve who have accused him of credit card theft. And because of that and related incidents I have had to fire two of our employees."

"Credit card theft involving Deer Creek or Buddy's Place?" asked Lew.

"Both," said Ty. "I think it's fair to say the situation started at Deer Creek. We serve a limited breakfast and lunch daily in the main lodge and I did not know until several weeks ago that two of our waitresses had been hired by Chet to be hostesses here at Buddy's Place."

"You mean tend bar?" asked Lew.

"No, they *hosted*," said Ty, putting an emphasis on the word *hosted*. "I'm told they worked from nine in the evening until whenever their patrons went home." He paused before saying, "Or when they went home with the patron."

"Home being the men's rooms or cottages at the preserve?" asked Lew. Ty nodded and coughed. Karen crossed her arms as she listened, her eyes calm. Osborne could see she had heard all this before.

"I get the picture," said Lew. "And how long has this been going on?"

"I'm told it started right after Chet opened the club nine months ago. From noon to nine he ran videos for customers. You can imagine the nature of those. And after nine? Live action."

"Wait," said Lew, "how is Buddy's Place connected to Deer Creek? Does the Deer Creek Preserve own this property?"

"No, no," said Wallis. "Gosh, no. But there is a history of Deer Creek members having owned this building in the past. Years ago the grandson of one of our founding members bought the land and built the Long Lake Supper Club, which offered entertainment. That was in the heyday of supper clubs in the Northwoods. But it's been closed for years.

"My understanding is Chet and a couple of his hunting buddies at Deer Creek talked over the possibility of renovating the building and turning it into a high-class gentlemen's club."

"There's an oxymoron for you," said Lew with a snort. Osborne had to turn away so no one could see the grin he couldn't resist.

"I can understand their thinking," said Ty. "Use of Deer Creek is ninety percent male. We don't have many ladies anxious to spend weeks up north fishing and hunting. In fact, during deer season there is an unwritten rule that women are not allowed."

"Excuse me, Ty," said Osborne, interrupting, "if it's okay with Chief Ferris, I have a question before you go any further."

Lew nodded as she said, "Karen, Mr. Wallis—I've deputized Dr. Osborne to help with the coroner's report and with this investigation. With his background in dental forensics he has been very helpful in the past with victim identification. Our official Loon Lake coroner, Irv Pecore, is being treated at St. Mary's Emergency Room after hitting a deer on his way here. I'm fortunate that Dr. Osborne could get here as soon as he has.

"I have two forensic experts from the Wausau Crime Lab on their way to help out as well. I expect them in an hour or so. One of those gentlemen will be taking the victims down to the crime lab facilities where autopsies will be performed. In the meantime, Dr. Osborne has authority from me to make any inquiries he thinks might help determine what has happened here."

"So that's why you're here, Dr. Osborne," said Karen. "I was wondering."

What Lew didn't add was that ever since the first time she had asked Osborne to step in as deputy coroner when Pecore was unavailable (most often due to being overserved and still under the influence), she had found his listening skills to be invaluable. Listening with ears and eyes was a talent Osborne had honed over thirty years of practicing dentistry and trying to deduce which toothaches were real, which were the peeves of hypochondriacs, and which might be better treated by an ear, nose, and throat specialist.

Comparing notes after the first time they had conducted an interrogation together she had found herself saying, "But, Doc, I didn't hear that."

"Lew," he had said that day, "you heard the answers to your questions. I listened between the lines. Not just to what they said but what I could see in their eyes and body language."

No longer hesitating to deputize Osborne when she anticipated difficulty getting information from witnesses or people under suspicion of having committed a crime, she had grown to appreciate the difference between what a man hears and what a woman hears: they made a good team in the interrogation room.

"My question, Ty," said Osborne, "is this: Are you saying that Chet Wright has been running an after-hours private club for certain well-to-do members of the Deer Creek Fishing and Hunting Preserve?"

"Not exactly," said Ty. "Initially, the members who encouraged Chet to open Buddy's Place wanted a place nearby where they could drink as much as they want and not have to drive afterward. So as far as I know Buddy's Place has been open to the general public. The problem is what started to happen after several of Chet's friends became regulars and certain promises were made."

"Promises that might include more intimate surroundings?" asked Lew.

"Yes," said Wallis. "Took a couple months before the three members in question started seeing charges on their credit cards that they couldn't recall making. To the tune of hundreds, even thousands of dollars.

"Before they came to me to complain, they approached Chet. He had photos that one of the women had taken while the men were inebriated. Chet tried to say that it wasn't his fault if they drank too much or used drugs when they were with the women. They were responsible for the charges and if they made any noise about it, he would call their wives."

"Pete Kretzler was robbed of over a hundred thousand dollars," said Karen.

"Kretzler, the surgeon from Milwaukee?" asked Osborne.

"Then there's Jud Westerman from Chicago. He's in commodities. Chet got him for sixty grand and, of course, there's Bert Bronk, whose family started one of the drugstore chains you see all over the Midwest," said Ty.

"That jerk hasn't ever been able to keep his pants on," said Karen. "His wife told me that's been going on for years.

"Chief Ferris," said Karen, "the long and short of it is Chet has been trying to defraud three of his best friends." She glanced at Wallis as she said, "Correct me if I'm wrong, Ty, but the way it worked is the two women would get them drunk—or drugged—then take compromising photos while charging their credit cards for alcohol and food."

"And threatening to tell their wives if they complained? Sounds like blackmail to me," said Lew.

"Call it what you will but Chet has been desperate these last few months," said Karen. "He lost all our money gambling and thought he could cover it up if he made more here. 'Course his plan was to take the profits from the club, then double and triple them at the casino. You can imagine how well that worked."

Lew turned to Ty Wallis. "Why haven't you reported this to me or to the county sheriff? This is blatant criminal activity; who are the women involved? I want names and contact information. I want the same information on the Deer Creek members, too."

"Of course," said Ty, shoulders slumping as he thrust his fists deeper into his pants pockets and rocked back and forth on the balls of his feet. "Guess I knew this was going to happen. I know I should have blown the whistle weeks ago when the whole nasty business came out. But . . ."

"But what?" asked Lew. "You better have a good 'but.'"

Chapter Eleven

"Maybe I made a wrong decision," said Ty in a rueful voice. "But as more details came out and the worse it got, I thought it best to keep the whole business as quiet as possible. I mean, these are family men. Think how this would look in the press."

"Now, Ty," said Karen, her eyebrows raised as she spoke with a soft urgency, "if I were you I'd tell Chief Ferris the *real* reason you didn't report Chet to the police."

Flashing Karen a look of annoyance, Ty grimaced. "All right, all right, I'm getting there, okay?" Another long pause, then a shrug of surrender: "I don't call the shots. I just work for these people—"

"These people? What people exactly?" asked Lew.

"Chet, the membership of the Deer Creek Preserve, the three guys who got bilked—all of 'em. I take orders. I hire who they tell me to hire." He shot a quick look at Karen before adding, "I do what they tell me and the three guys whose cards were overbilled told me in no uncertain way to 'take care of it and keep my goddamn mouth shut.' In exactly those words. And believe you me these are men who have gotten away with a lot worse than this."

At the sight of Lew's questioning eyes, he added, "Not while I've been working here, but there are things I've been told that happened in the past."

He paused then, coughed, cleared his throat, and said, "Something else I need you to know. Right or wrong, I need this job. My real-estate business over in Three Lakes went bust two years ago, I got two kids in high school, my wife left me . . ." Osborne could see the poor guy was on the verge of tears. "I don't have to tell you, Chief Ferris, it can be real hard to make a living up here . . . sorry. But if I've broken any laws it's just . . . I'm just trying to keep it together, y'know?"

"I see," said Lew. "Thank you for being honest, Ty, and you haven't broken any laws that I can see. But that's enough for right now. We can talk more about this later. At the moment I need you to tell me about the women. Who are they and how can I reach them?"

"Well," Ty said with a heavy exhale as he pointed up at the piano, "you've got one right there. Tiffany Niedermeier. The other woman who has been in on the scam is Nina Krezminski. I can give you an address and phone number for her. But if you need next of kin information on Tiffany, her mother lives in Rhinelander. At least that's what my secretary told me before Karen and I walked over here.

"As far as I know Tiffany isn't married. No children. Again, not that I'm aware anyway. Niedermeier is her maiden name if that helps."

"I'll check on the mother, Chief Ferris," said Osborne.

"Thank you, Doc," said Lew. "Once you find her address and as soon as Bruce gets here, you and I better drive over to inform her of her daughter's death. I hate to deliver news like that by myself and I would hate to have her hear the news from the media."

Turning back to Ty Wallis, Lew said, "What is the status right now of the credit card billings? Do the banks know about this?"

"No. The men involved wanted to keep the banks out of it. They hoped that if Chet paid everyone back that it wouldn't have to go any further than my office."

"And has that happened?" asked Lew. "Has Chet paid back the money? What's the total owed to all three men?"

"One hundred seventy-eight thousand and thirty-two cents. He was supposed to have three checks here today. I have a meeting scheduled at three o'clock and—"

Lew cut him off. "So the three of you—I mean four including you—thought you could sweep all this under the table with no questions asked? And what about the two ladies? Was that action going to continue? There is a word for that, you know: prostitution. It's a criminal offense."

"May I answer that?" asked Karen, raising her right hand like a schoolgirl. "Men like Chet and his friends think their money entitles them to do whatever they wish, whenever they wish, and to whomever they wish.

"Took me a few years to understand that and you can call me stupid. But just so you know Chet never said a word to me about any of this. If he had I might have saved everyone from a big surprise.

"You see, it didn't matter *what* Chet said he would do because he couldn't. There is no one hundred seventy-eight thousand dollars and thirty-two cents. Chet has lost every dime we ever had. He's been lying to everyone."

"It can't be that bad, Karen," said Osborne, stunned. "You can't mean *everything* is gone? Your house alone is worth over a million dollars—"

"Nine point five to be exact, Dr. Osborne."

"And the lake property that Chet inherited. It's all gone?"

"House, land, vehicles—mortgaged to the hilt. Until this morning when Ty called to tell me Chet was dead, I've been trying to salvage enough money to live on. And I've been in meetings myself with two lawyers: one for my divorce and another for bankruptcy." She gave a weak smile.

"At least Chet's dying will save me having to pay the divorce lawyer more than what I owe him so far." After a brief pause, she said, "And unless someone else steps up there won't even be a funeral. I can't pay for one."

"Boy oh boy, I find this hard to believe," said Osborne, shaking his head as he spoke. He pursed his lips before saying, "Karen, I'm sorry to ask a personal question but since I know both your folks are gone, how are you managing?"

Good question, thought Lew. She was wondering if the woman could afford to buy food.

"Right now I am doing okay. Hidden away in our attic was an antique doll collection that Chet's mother left to me. Chet had forgotten all about that collection, thank heavens, or he would have pawned that, too. I was able to sell it on an antiques website for enough money to go back to school.

"I have a degree in education and quite a few of the photos I've taken over the years have won awards. So this fall I'm starting work on an MFA while teaching photography at the tech college in Rhinelander. It isn't much but enough to live on. Once I finish graduate school, I'm pretty sure I can get a tenured teaching position . . . somewhere . . . I hope."

"It's that bad?" asked Osborne. Karen's eyes glimmered with tears and all she could do was nod.

From the table near the entrance where he had been sitting with Joyce, the head of maintenance for Deer Creek stood up. It was obvious he had been listening. He walked over and put an arm around Karen's shoulders. A slender man of modest height, he couldn't be more than an inch taller than Karen. Aside from the lines in their faces, standing side by side, they resembled two teenagers.

"KayKay, want me to drive you home? We're old friends," explained Fred Smith to the questioning eyes around him. "We grew up next door to each other. Karen's known me since I was this high"—he held his free hand at knee level—"before kindergarten even. Come on, KayKay," he said with a squeeze of her shoulders, "one of these days it'll all be okay. Like it used to be, right?"

"Thanks, Fred," said Karen, patting the hand he had placed on her right shoulder and raising grateful eyes to his. "Certainly can't get worse, can it? Or . . . ," she said after a pause, "maybe it can."

"Chief Ferris," said Fred, "just so you know, I kept warning Chet that piano was a hazard. Now we got this accident. I can't tell you how many times I told him something like this would happen. It's a shame, just a shame." Osborne couldn't decide if Smith had the mannerisms of an old biddy or a sad-eyed golden retriever.

"Thank you, Mr. Smith. I appreciate your input and I'll be talking to you later," said Lew, anxious to get him out of the way.

"Karen," said Osborne, "I'm sure Chief Ferris will have more questions for you but right now I need specifics for the death certificate for your husband. Do you mind taking a chair and going over a few details with me?" He pulled out a chair from a nearby table. "Shouldn't take more than a few minutes and I'm sorry, but it has to be done and the sooner the better."

"Of course, Dr. Osborne, but first I do have one last question for Ty." Looking at the manager, she asked, "With Chet dead do you think Pete and Jud and Bert will be expecting me to pay them the money Chet owes? I mean, I know legally I have just inherited Chet's problems but weren't they close friends of his? Each one has more money than God and once they know I'm nearly bankrupt?"

"I have no idea," said Ty, waving the world away with one hand as his shoulders slumped. "I may never know because I'm going to lose my job over this."

"No, you won't, Ty Wallis," said Lew. "If you've been honest with me about these shenanigans—and I think you have—I will make it clear to those gentlemen that the only way to keep their names out of the press going forward will be to cooperate with our investigation. Cooperation is critical if the Deer Creek Fishing and Hunting Preserve wants to salvage their reputation in the midst of this mess."

Ty threw her a doubtful glance. "I hope you're right."

"I'm not right, I'm serious. If any one of those three men gives you any trouble," said Lew, "you call me ASAP. They should have reported the fraud the moment they saw it happening and not have enlisted you to cover up their foolishness."

A loud knocking on the wall near the hallway caused everyone to turn around. A tall, gangly man in khaki fishing shorts, a red T-shirt, and two cameras with long zoom lenses slung around his neck stood waving at them. Bright dark brown eyes over a full head of auburn curls with sideburns that met in a tangled full beard gave him the air of a friendly bear loping their way.

"Where do you want me to start, Chief Ferris?" asked the man, an individual familiar to Osborne and Lew, as he walked through the Entertainment Center. He had long, tan legs that seemed never to end. Osborne's buddies at McDonald's liked to kid the thirty-two-year-old college dropout that his lower appendages entered a room at least a day before the rest of his long, lanky body.

"Better that than your beer bellies," Ray would respond with a cheerful wink.

As he neared, it was easy to read the bold white lettering on his T-shirt:

Romance, Excitement, and Live Bait

Get it all fishing with Ray

"What is *he* doing here?" Before anyone could say a word, Ty Wallis was racing across the room shouting, "Goddammit, I told you to stay off the preserve property—"

"Hold on," said Lew, running after Ty and grabbing him by one arm, "this is one of my deputies, Ray Pradt. He's here to help with the investigation."

"A *deputy*? This commode a *deputy*? You got to be kidding me." Ty's face was turning redder by the minute. "I've kicked this . . . this . . . whoever he is . . . off our lakes so many times. Do you have *any* idea how many of our trophy walleyes he's poached?"

"Yes," said Lew, "I believe I do. But Buddy's Place is not on the Deer Creek Preserve. It may be a crime scene and I have deputized this man. So, Ty, please settle down. Ray is the best tracker north of Mexico and I may need his eyes and ears today."

Ty's eyes widened as she spoke and turning back to stare at the elevated piano, he said, "You mean this wasn't an accident?"

"I'm not sure yet," said Lew, "but I've observed enough this morning that I've had good reason to request the expertise of both the Wausau Crime Lab and Ray Pradt so I can be sure that we get an accurate picture of what happened here."

"But this idiot—"

"I know, I know," said Lew. "Please, be assured I know who I am working with and why. Now if you will leave us alone, I need to give direction here."

Reaching for her walkie-talkie, she buzzed Roger. "Officer Adamczak, would you please come into the main room here? I'd like you to escort all the folks here out to the foyer so I can speak in private with Ray and Doc. Thank you."

Grudgingly, Ty Wallis joined Fred, Joyce, and Karen to head down the hallway with Roger. Watching them go, Osborne caught Lew's eye. They exchanged a hint of a smile. Neither of them could blame Ty for his frustration with Osborne's neighbor.

The misdemeanor file on Ray Pradt was one that Police Chief Lewellyn Ferris sometimes felt she kept for entertainment. His record of poaching on private water extended back to when he was age ten and her predecessor had questioned him one morning after he had begged to have a trophy walleye he had caught displayed in the windowed ice chest that sat on the sidewalk outside Ralph's Sporting Goods.

"Tell me, son, where did you catch that fish?" asked the chief of the Loon Lake Police, peering into the ice chest at the impressive fish. "I haven't seen a walleye that big since old man Carstenson stocked his pond. Sure you weren't fishing over at his place?"

Ray had made the mistake of taking a young neighbor, Robbie, fishing with him that morning. Robbie, only eight years old, was standing guard at the ice chest and so excited to have been fishing with his hero that when he heard the police officer's question, he jumped to answer. Before Ray could say a word, Robbie had piped up, "Oh, Chief Sloan, it was so exciting. I got one, too, but not as big as Ray's."

"Really"—the chief of police had turned to Robbie—"remember where that was?"

"Sure do. We rode our bikes out to Perch Lake Road, turned right, and then we just followed the *No Trespassing* signs." Robbie's grin faded when he saw his good buddy invited to take a ride in the officer's squad car.

While Ray never lost his proclivity for finding fine fish in all the wrong places, in his twenties and timed with the launch of his guiding service, he learned to avoid most felony behavior patterns: He kept his indulgence in cannabis to a minimum and a dangerous dalliance with alcohol was cut short thanks to a stint in rehab. On the other hand, his addiction to dumb jokes never abated.

What made him valuable to the Loon Lake Police Department, in spite of the poaching relapses, was his talent for tracking bear, deer, grouse—and humans (lost, fleeing, or catastrophically down on their luck, as in dead)—through the forests of northern

Wisconsin. The McDonald's coffee crowd might boo his jokes but no one challenged the fact that he had the eyes of an eagle.

Ray may have been born into one of Loon Lake's "good families," the son of a respected physician with an older brother who became a surgeon and a sister who was a renowned litigator in Chicago, and destined for an Ivy League education, but it was the lakes, rivers, and tall timbers that filled his heart. He survived high school only to flunk out of college. Happily.

Instead he spent his late teens and twenties harvesting wisdom from the old hermits who lived down back roads, men who had learned that the secret for surviving nature at her angriest was to live in solitude and subsist on what they could catch, shoot, or trap. And so it was that Ray Pradt found himself mentored by the shrewdest trackers in the Northwoods: men as cunning as their prey. He never forgot a lesson.

While the misdemeanor file expanded over time the new pages benefited the Loon Lake Police in an unexpected way: Ray strayed far enough from what was legal by game warden standards that he earned familiarity if not a dubious respect from other miscreants; i.e. a pipeline of contacts privy to truth behind rumor.

When Roger's group had disappeared down the hall, Ray turned to Lew and said, "Sorry, Chief, didn't mean to upset that guy."

"Forget it," said Lew, "and don't worry about taking photos. Bruce Peters is on his way up from Wausau with one of his colleagues. They can handle photographing the scene here.

"What I need you to do is . . ." She paused and motioned for Osborne to join her and Ray at the far side of the room. After walking Ray to the front of the Entertainment Center, Lew explained what he would find on the piano once he went up the narrow stairway.

"Please do not touch or move a thing," she reminded him. "The Wausau boys are on their way and Bruce wants nothing disturbed.

Nothing. That's why I haven't had the piano lowered beyond where the EMTs left it."

Ray nodded in understanding. "Hey, so our man, Bruce, will be up? I owe him an afternoon on my boat once this fishing tournament is over. Tell that razzbonya to hang around, will you?"

"Good luck with that," said Lew. "He's got his work cut out here. Now, Ray"—she pointed to the footprints on the workbench—"see those? I need you to see if you can find more outside."

"I see, I see, and say . . . not . . . another word."

Raising his right hand, Ray spoke in a pattern of pausing before uttering critical words: a pattern designed, Osborne was convinced, to hold his audience hostage until he deigned to deliver valuable insights (valuable by his standards, that is). "I . . . will scour . . . the landscape. Lucky for you . . . it rained hard two days ago so . . . chances are . . . we got g-o-o-o-d sign out there. If . . . there is sign . . . to be . . . got.

"But . . . I want to shoot those footprints. I'll need an image for comparison . . . with what I may . . . or may not . . . find . . . outdoors. Is that okay?"

"Of course," said Lew.

Ray checked his watch. "Whoops. Got to be somewhere pretty darn soon. I'll get to work right away."

Funny, thought Osborne, when Ray had a deadline in *his* world his speech sped up. Oh well.

"I got a meeting with my fishing team at five this afternoon," said Ray.

"Say, Doc"—he turned to Osborne, who was waiting at the bottom of the stairs—"you'll have Mason out at my place by four, won't you? I have to show her the tackle, tell her what her job is. Did you know she's working for me?"

"She'll be there," said Osborne, not sure how he was going to manage that and meet with Tiffany Niedermeier's mother, but he knew he'd have to make it work somehow.

Lew must have seen the expression on his face. "I'll make sure Doc has her there on time."

"Okay." Ray stepped off the stairs with a final glance up. "So that's Tiffany Niedermeier, huh. Jeez . . . last time I saw her she was dancing at Thunder Bay with no visible means of upper-body support. Wonder what she was doing here?"

Chapter Twelve

Walking out of the building with Ray, Lew and Osborne were greeted with a scene of controlled chaos: though Roger and his four charges remained inside the foyer, outside was the crowd of bystanders, which had doubled since Lew had arrived. Added to the increasing number of people and vehicles was a large SUV from the local television station.

Lew waved away a woman reporter carrying a microphone and in the midst of setting up a tripod for her camera with a simple, "Sorry, miss. Not till we've notified next of kin. We're still trying to find out what happened here." She turned her head to one side and muttered under her breath to Osborne, "So much for Ty wanting to keep this out of the press."

She was in the midst of saying, "No, I am not at this time prepared to make an official statement of any kind—" when an unmarked car followed by a large white unmarked van pulled into the parking lot beside her police cruiser: Bruce Peters, a colleague named Rich, and the two men who would retrieve the victims' bodies had arrived.

"Welcome to Loon Lake," said Lew to the newcomers as she herded them into the building and away from inquisitive ears. "This is one of our top tourist attractions: Buddy's Place. I'm kidding. It's a gentlemen's club that has only been open a few months."

Once inside she gave all four men a brief description of what they would find in the Entertainment Center and the names of the victims. After walking them down the hallway to the Entertainment Center, she and Osborne stood quietly at the back of the room while the four took in the scene. "No one has moved that piano since you got here, correct?" asked Bruce.

"With the exception of Joe Teske, the paramedic who wore gloves and lowered it enough to be sure he didn't have an injured individual needing emergency transport, the answer is yes—no one has moved it, Bruce."

On hearing her answer, Rich moved forward with his camera to begin documenting the layout of the room while Lew used her walkie-talkie to ask Roger to send Joyce down the hall to meet with them.

When Joyce arrived Lew motioned toward Bruce as she said, "Joyce, this is Bruce Peters and he is a senior forensics expert with the Wausau Crime Lab. He will have plenty of questions for you so please share everything you know.

"Bruce, this is Joyce Harmon. She is the janitor for Buddy's Place and the Deer Creek Fishing and Hunting Preserve next door. Joyce cleans here in the mornings and called this in right after she arrived this morning. She is also the person who knows the most about the operation of the piano. She handles all the maintenance on it. Correct, Joyce?" The woman nodded.

"One of the men back in the foyer with Officer Adamczak, the guy with the buzz cut wearing dark green, is Joyce's boss. That's Fred Smith and he is the head of maintenance for the Deer Creek Preserve and this place." Lew dropped her voice. "My guess is Joyce does all the work here."

"Good, good," said Bruce, eyebrows bouncing with excitement.

A tall, muscular man in his late thirties, he was clean-cut but with black hair and a thick black mustache that matched heavy eyebrows: eyebrows that refused to hide what he was thinking. "You would make a terrible undercover cop," Lew once told him. "I can tell what you're thinking just by watching those eyebrows jump." But if Bruce's feelings were at times too transparent, his attention to detail was impeccable.

"First thing, Mrs. Harmon—" he said with a notebook out as he faced Joyce.

"Joyce, just call me Joyce."

"All right, Joyce, if you will wait over there." He motioned to a nearby table. "I see Chief Ferris has marked off a walkway for us so we won't contaminate anything and if you will wait there, I'll be over to get your prints right away."

"Why?" Joyce looked alarmed. "*I* haven't done anything."

"Didn't Chief Ferris say you know how to operate the hoist for the piano?"

"Well, yes but—"

"I will need your prints in order to determine who is the most recent person to have raised or lowered the piano as well as someone who is *expected* to have operated the apparatus on a regular basis. Isn't it likely you raised and lowered the piano while lubricating it or maybe just cleaning things up recently?"

"Yes, of course. I lubricated the pulleys last Saturday."

"Well, then, I need your fingerprints. Does your boss work with the piano?"

"No, never."

"Excuse me, Bruce," said Lew, reaching for his arm to pull him off to one side of the room and away from Joyce. She motioned for him to bend down so she could speak low enough to keep their conversation out of Joyce's hearing. "One more thing—the other man waiting in the foyer with Roger, besides Fred Smith, is the manager of the Deer Creek Fishing and Hunting Preserve and the woman standing with them is the widow of . . ." And she pointed up at the piano. "Doc needs to get information from her for the death certificate. Is it okay if I leave you here with Joyce while Doc and I take care of that?"

"Please tell her that I'll need to see her when you're finished," said Bruce.

"Will do. Then after we finish with Karen Wright, Bruce, Doc and I have to leave to notify the mother of the female victim of the fact her daughter is no longer alive. That has to happen as soon as possible. Not sure how long that will take but I'll return immediately afterward.

"In the meantime, I have instructed Ray Pradt to secure a one-mile radius around this property."

Bruce's eyebrows shot up. "Why is that?"

"S-s-h," said Lew, urging him to lower his voice. "You'll see when you look behind the curtain over there to the right. We found sandy footprints on top of the workbench that's up against the outside wall and under the window. Could be old but I think the sand looks like it might still be wet. Hard for me to tell."

Outside again, Lew saw Ray studying the terrain around the large trash bins. She heard him call to Osborne, who was about to follow her in his car. "Don't forget, Doc, I have to have Mason at my place by four if not earlier, okay?" Osborne waved assurance as he climbed into his Subaru.

Irene Niedermeier lived on the west side of Rhinelander on a street of homes built nearly a hundred years ago for executives at the paper mill, homes significantly larger, grander, than the boxy single-story ones six blocks away and destined for mill laborers. Those houses hugged the loading zones and cowered under fumes not yet regulated by the EPA.

A paved walkway wound past a border of blooming white and coral impatiens and led to a heavy wooden door set inside rock and stone walls and tucked snugly under a cedar-shingled roof: an elegant façade. Lew reached for the brass lion's head adorning the door and knocked. The woman who answered was as elegant as her home.

She had the prominent cheekbones and fair skin that signaled Scandinavian heritage. Her silver hair was pulled tight into a bun with not a wisp out of place. She wore light makeup, a pale blue dress, modest beige heels, and simple gold studs in her ears. She impressed Osborne as someone who dressed with care every day and kept a pristine household. He wasn't sure they had the right house.

"I'm sorry," said the woman before Lew could open her mouth, "but don't you see that sign in the yard? *No solicitors.*" With a firm push, she shut the door so hard it nearly hit Lew in the face. Lew knocked again.

"What is it?"

Setting all etiquette aside, Lew spoke fast. "I am Lewellyn Ferris, chief of the Loon Lake Police, and I am here about your daughter."

The woman stared at her for a brief instant before saying, "I don't have a daughter." The door shut.

"I better check the address again, Lew. Sorry about this," said Osborne as they walked back toward their cars. They hadn't gone twenty feet when the door opened behind them.

"All right," said the woman in a blunt tone. "That's not the case, but I haven't seen my daughter in twenty years. Well," she shifted her eyes to one side, "that's not exactly true either. She did call me a few years ago. But she didn't come to her father's funeral and I don't want to see her. If she's in trouble that's her problem."

Lew walked back up to the entryway saying, "She's not in trouble. May Dr. Osborne and I come in for a few minutes? We have important personal news to share with you. You are Irene Niedermeier, mother of Tiffany Niedermeier—am I correct?"

With a sigh, the woman stepped back and held the door open. "I guess. Please come in." They followed her into a small but tasteful living room with a brocade sofa and matching armchairs facing a stone fireplace. "You can sit there," she said, pointing to the straight-backed sofa.

Lew leaned forward with her elbows on her knees, her eyes intent on the woman's face. "I deeply regret having to tell you that your daughter, Tiffany, died in an apparent accident either last night or early this morning."

"Where?"

"Here in Loon Lake near the Deer Creek Fishing and Hunting Preserve in a club called Buddy's Place. We do not yet know the cause of death because we have to have an autopsy done."

"Why? How much will that cost me?"

The question caught Lew off-guard. "Well because I said an '*apparent* accident,' there is a question that it may be a double homicide."

Irene Niedermeier gave Lew a calculating look. "A *double* homicide? How does that happen? You can only die once."

Her comment was so sarcastic that Osborne couldn't help himself. "You don't seem too upset, Mrs. Niedermeier."

"Oh, golly." The woman looked off to her right and out a side window before saying, "I'm sure you think I'm cruel and unfeeling, but I have been expecting this news for years . . . years . . . years." Her voice ran up and down as she repeated the word *years*. She glanced down at her hands, which were in her lap. "I imagine I have to explain myself, don't I?"

"Only if you feel you can," said Lew.

"Tiffany was born mean," said her mother. "Don't ask me how that happens but she was mean as a baby, mean as young girl. Just plain mean."

"Is she your only child?" asked Osborne.

"No. She had a sister, Claudette, who was three years younger. When Claudette was five and learning to ride her bike, she was killed in a traffic accident. Right out there in front of our house."

Irene stood up as she talked and walked over to the window that looked out at the street in front of the house. She pointed as she said, "Right there. I was in the kitchen frosting her birthday cake. My husband, Per, had walked back to the garage for a minute or two. He was helping Claudette get started. She had training wheels and everything when somehow she ended up out in the street in front of an oncoming car."

"Was her sister nearby?" asked Lew, sensing she knew the answer even as she asked the question.

"Oh yes. She was right there. You don't need to ask me how I think it happened."

Lew and Osborne sat silent.

"I would like details from you if that's okay," said Irene. "Was Tiffany in a car accident or—"

"Nothing like that," said Lew with a quick look at Osborne.

"Grim as it is, I would tell Irene everything we know," said Osborne.

With that Lew gave her a description of what had been discovered on the piano early that morning. She made no mention of the footprints but she did say that Chet Wright was separated from his wife and had been experiencing financial difficulties.

"I don't know if it helps you folks," said Irene when Lew had finished, "but you should know that Tiffany ran away when she was sixteen. Before her father died, he hired a private detective so we were able to learn that she was working as a stripper and a call girl in Las Vegas.

"That was in her twenties. She would be thirty-seven now. Anyway, the man we hired reported that she had a drug problem and had been dealing drugs, too, until things went wrong and she got beat up. Badly. The last we heard was she got out of the drug dealing but I don't know that for sure.

"Her father died five years ago. He never gave up hoping she'd at least call, but only time I heard from her was two years ago when she was destitute. She wanted money."

"Did you send her any?" Lew's question hung in the air.

"No. No, I didn't. Can you imagine how it feels to a parent to have a daughter who dances in strip joints? Really, can you?"

"Actually," said Lew, "I can. When my daughter got out of high school and needed money for college, she got hired to dance out at the Thunder Bay Bar. I was doing my best to help her finance her education but I was working as a secretary at the mill and going to school nights myself so money was really tight."

"Where is she today?" asked Irene.

"Milwaukee. Suzanne got a degree in accounting and today she runs her own accounting firm."

"Do you ever wonder how she avoided the dark side of that business?" asked Irene.

"First, I was supportive. I knew she could make better money as a dancer than waiting tables or working a call center. And we were struggling together."

What Lew didn't add was that she loved Suzanne with all her heart, that she had confidence in her daughter that together they could make it through the hard times, and she made sure to tell her that. Often.

"I'm glad life works out for some people," said Irene with a heavy sigh. She attempted a smile.

"I need to ask you a few questions for the death certificate," said Osborne, "but before that Chief Ferris and I would be happy to call a friend or another family member to help you handle this today. Maybe a priest or a minister?"

"Oh no, I'm fine," said Irene. "You must understand: Tiffany's death is a relief. I used to have nightmares that she might crawl in a window some night and, well, you know . . ."

Osborne did not know. He didn't want to know.

Chapter Thirteen

Shortly after two that afternoon Osborne found himself driving crosstown from Irene Niedermeier's house to his daughter's. Even though he hadn't had lunch yet, he'd decided to stop to be sure that Mason had her waders and was ready to head out to his place. She didn't have to be at Ray's for another hour or so but if she was home and ready, it would save him an extra trip into town to pick her up.

"He-l-l-o, anybody home?" he called through the front porch screen door of the old Victorian where Erin's family lived.

"In the kitchen, Dad. Door's open, c'mon back." Erin, the younger of his two daughters, was leaning over the old oak table where she was rolling out a pie crust. "Rhubarb pie, Dad. Come for dinner later?"

He watched his daughter as she bent forward, arms working. One long blonde braid hung down in front of her right shoulder so close to the top of the flattened pie dough that Osborne reached to hold it out of the way.

"Thanks, Dad, you arrived at a critical moment," said Erin with a grin as she rolled the pie crust onto the rolling pin, then unrolled it onto the heap of fresh rhubarb slices glistening in the pie plate and stabbed it with a fork to let steam out as it baked. "God forbid

I commit a food felony and leave a hair in my pie. Hold on while I shove this sucker in the oven."

"I stopped by to pick up Mason if she's ready," said Osborne. "She needs to be at Ray's by three thirty. She can hang out at my place until then."

"Right. I need to talk to you about that. I'm not sure this is such a good idea."

"Why not?" Osborne was taken aback. "If you ask me, the kid's thrilled about it. He is paying her, you know."

"Did she tell you what the schedule is? Ray wants Mason to meet him and those boys at the dock at five in the morning and again at eight thirty at night until who knows how late." Erin had picked up a tea towel and was wiping off her hands.

"Oh . . . ," said Osborne with a pause, "I didn't know the schedule. But I see Ray's thinking: have the boys fish as early and as late as tournament regulations allow. Makes sense to me. Best times to go after muskies."

"Well, it's not a good time for eleven-year-old girls who need their sleep. Plus I have to drive Cody down to Madison for a soccer camp and Beth wants to tour the campus so I'm taking all three kids and we'll stay overnight with my friend, Bridget. You remember Bridget?"

"Erin," said Osborne, "you are going to break that child's heart."

Erin threw her towel on the counter. "C'mon, Dad, be reasonable. She's a little girl. Plus who knows what kind of language those college boys use. Not only that: Mason told me Ray wants her to help pick out rap music for them to listen to on the boat. Have you heard rap music? Dad, it's full of . . . of . . . bad language."

"It's only three days, kiddo, and I'll be right there. Why don't we have her stay overnight at my place? I'll take her over in the mornings and I will be waiting when the boat comes in at night. How about that?"

"Umm." Erin struggled with his suggestion. "Well . . . okay, Dad. But on one condition—she has to keep her phone with her all the time. Okay? That way she can call you if they're running late or something."

What she didn't say but Osborne knew was her worry was that Ray might get into some of his usual mischief and forget he had a young girl nearby. Osborne had to agree with her concern: two college boys plus Ray Pradt? That could be a recipe for bad behavior.

On the other hand, Ray had been quite pleased to have been selected as one of the team coaches. If his college team won or placed in the top five, he stood to make good money, plus the boat company sponsoring the boys would be likely to hire him again. Osborne was confident his good friend and neighbor was not likely to screw up. Not this time anyway.

"Are you sure about her keeping the phone with her all the time? She'll be right next door . . ." He had been surprised at Mason's birthday party when her parents gave her a smartphone worth several hundred dollars. He didn't say anything at the time but he thought it pretty indulgent for an eleven-year-old.

"I'll loan her one of my waterproof cases," said Osborne. "I can just see that phone going in the water."

"Still, Dad, I'm not sure about this . . . Wait, I have an idea. Why don't you make it a point of helping Mason out? That way you could be with her while she's down at Ray's. That would make me feel a whole lot better."

"And I wish I could but I can't—and I think you'll understand why," said Osborne. "You have to keep what I'm about to tell you confidential until it's official, but Lew got quite the nine-one-one call this morning. Pecore hit a deer on his way out to the scene so Lew deputized me to help with the death certificates and . . ."

He gave Erin a quick description of the macabre tableau at Buddy's Place, ending with, ". . . so it's still too soon to know if it was an accident or homicide but Mark's office will be notified ASAP if it's the latter."

It had been a year since Erin's husband, Mark, had been elected district attorney after a brief, frustrating year in private practice. Erin liked to joke that he preferred genuine crimes over the imaginary ones cited in contentious divorces.

Erin whistled. "Wow. Chet Wright, huh. This will make the Chicago papers. And Tiffany Niedermeier? Well, that doesn't surprise me."

"You know her?"

"Who doesn't? But that's because I'm married to the DA. We hear all the good stuff. Yes, I know about Tiffany, though I've never met her. Word is she's an expert on the bedroom ceilings of men with money. Loon Lake money, that is.

"But, Dad, if you're going to be working with Chief Ferris on a case that big, will you be able to keep an eye on Mason?"

"Of course. I'll make sure that I'm around when she needs me. Come on, Erin," said Osborne, reaching for his daughter's hand to give her a reassuring squeeze, "you know that kid will be so disappointed if you put the kibosh on this."

"Well . . . all right then." With that Erin shouted up the stairway in the direction of the kids' bedrooms for Mason to pack an overnight bag and get ready to leave with her grandfather.

"So Ryan and Jake, have you heard the story about the genie and the two muskie fishermen?" asked Ray with a wink at the two college boys who were anxious to get their marching orders for the fishing tournament. Osborne had arrived with Mason fifteen minutes earlier and decided to listen in on the meeting with the boys. He wanted to be sure that Mason would not be asked to do more than she could handle.

At the moment, however, he was worried that Ray was about to go too far with one of his off-color jokes. Those might be fine for college boys but not his granddaughter.

Mason was perched at one end of the long picnic table where Ray had set out the gear approved by the tournament officials. She looked tiny beside the two boys, who had to be at least six two or three and so muscled that Osborne suspected they spent hours at the gym.

Add Ray to the picture with his six-foot-six height and booming voice and Mason was dwarfed. On the other hand, she was glued to every word Ray said with such serious eyes that Osborne knew it would break her heart if he were to say she couldn't be the "gofer" for the crew. Still, this joke might be a deal breaker even if it was Ray's technique for bonding with his team.

". . . So the genie . . . appears to the fishermen and tells them . . . it's their lucky day. They get to have . . . one wish come true." With the promise of good news to come, Ray's voice grew louder as he said, "So . . . the two confab for a minute before one says . . . 'We want a lake full of beer.'"

Ryan and Jake chuckled. "'Done,' says the genie and waved his magic wand." Ray demonstrated the genie's action and his audience, including Mason, leaned forward in anticipation.

"Sure 'nough," said Ray, "the two fishermen found themselves . . . in their boat . . . bobbing . . . on a lake full of beer. 'Bad news, though,' said the genie . . ." Ray raised his right index finger and paused even longer than usual as the two boys and Mason waited for the denouement: "'Now you have to pee in the boat.'"

Oh jeez, thought Osborne, listening to the boys guffaw along with Ray. Mason had an uncertain grin on her face and her cheeks reddened. Osborne shot Ray a warning look: this better be the last one or you lose Mason.

"Not to worry, Doc," said Ray. "Not to worry, okay?" With that, he dropped the comedy act and—with no hostage-taking pauses—laid out the plan for the next three days.

"Okay, boys, I'm your coach and Mason here is our manager. Got that?" Mason's shoulders straightened up. "Among other things, she's going to keep our tackle clean and organized. So, Mason, tell the boys what lures they're going to be using."

"Sure," said Mason standing up. With that all five feet four inches of Osborne's granddaughter seemed to gain more height as she reached for three lures that had been set out on the table. "Coach Ray wants you to use exclusively this Rizzo Tail."

She held it high so they could see it. "It's solid white with a brass blade and that's because you'll be fishing on stained water. Any questions for Coach?"

Both boys nodded. "My dad fishes Rizzo Tails, too," said the boy named Ryan.

"Then there is this one, the Double Cowgirl."

Mason held up a lure Osborne had never used. It had ten blades and looked heavy. Good thing the boys were well muscled.

"And the last one is the Loudmouth." She held up a small chartreuse and brown–colored bait.

"But that's for bass," said the second boy, Jake. "Why will we use that?"

Mason turned to Ray who said, "Trust me, guys. It works for muskie and very few fishermen know how good it is. See, this plastic body is filled . . . filled . . . with steel shot. Damn thing makes so much noise. Hell, it's the loudest lure out there. Makes fish *want* to attack.

"Thank you, Mason. So Mason will be ready if we need her for lures, food, anything. While we are fishing, she will be on shore here or, if the weather turns bad, inside my place."

He pointed over to his house trailer, which was painted neon green, the head of a giant muskie anchoring one end with its mouth open wide to expose a row of needle-like teeth. The teeth, executed by an ex-girlfriend of Ray's, were highlighted with a silver paint that glowed menacingly in the afternoon sun. Ray took great pride in the tears of toddlers frightened by the sight of his masterpiece.

Continuing his instructions for the tournament, Ray said, "Mason will watch over the gear we can't fit into the boat, she'll keep track of our snacks, and . . . she might just pick out some tunes for us to have in the boat. Sound good to everyone? Any questions?"

Mason looked so proud and in charge that Osborne gave up any thought of telling her she couldn't take the job. He refused to be guilty of causing heartbreak.

"So, guys, you're next—Ryan, Jake. Here's the deal, we are going to do what the rest of our competitors won't do: we are going to fish early and fish late. By that I mean *real* early and *real* late. I want us on the dock here at five o'clock tomorrow morning. We'll break midday for lunch. Then back on the dock here at one thirty and we fish until eight."

Spotting the look on Osborne's face, he said, "Now, Doc, I don't expect Mason to be here every minute all day. But if she can have us set up by five thirty, once we head out, she's done for the morning. Evenings I expect she'll be home by nine, nine thirty at the latest."

"That's okay with me, Grandpa," said Mason, turning to him with eager eyes.

"Fine," said Osborne. "I have no problem with that schedule."

"Good, we got that set then," said Ray. "Now, boys, here's the big deal: no shore beating for us, no weed patches, not even reeds. *We are going for suspended muskies.*"

Confusion crossed the boys' faces. "That's because those big girls hunkered down deep are the biggest fish in this lake.

"Well, with one exception." He pointed to an offshore reed bed running a good 500 feet from end to end parallel to the shoreline. "We got old Buster right in there somewhere. She's fifty-plus inches and God knows how many pounds but no one has ever caught that mother. She's eaten more leaders and lines than you'll buy in your lifetime."

Mason raised her hand. "Honey, just speak up," said Ray. "You're the manager here. Yeah, what is it?"

"Why do you call her Buster if she's not a he?"

"I've seen that fish," said Ray, his voice low as if he worried that the monster muskellunge might hear him, "and I can tell you there is nothing feminine about that creature. Trust me, sweetie pie, when you see a fish that can eat you alive . . . Well, she is Buster to me."

The boys' eyes were big and Mason's jaw had dropped. Ray had them in thrall. Osborne had seen the legendary muskie himself, lost two crankbaits to her, and he had to admit that Ray was not exaggerating.

"Gear-wise," said Ray, "we'll be using eight-foot rods that I've fitted with new, quality reels that have excellent anti-reverse. You can thank our sponsor for those. I've fitted our rods with the new super lines, the ones with hundred-pound stretch and fluorocarbon leaders. None of these fifty-cent wire leaders for us. These new ones cost a lot more but they disappear in the water."

"They do?" asked Ryan. "That's cool, but how do you know the fish can't see 'em?"

"I trust experience and the fact that *I* can't see them. Since interviews with fish are rare, you'll just have to take my word for it. More questions, guys?"

The boys and Mason were quiet. "All righty, then," said Ray. "First thing in the morning, we're going to practice your figure eights. Mason, the boys know this but you might not unless your grandpa taught you. Muskies often follow your lure as you reel it in so you want to tip the rod down to pull that lure in a figure-eight motion by the side of the boat. Right, boys, you know that?" The boys nodded in agreement.

"What else do we know?" Again silence.

"Muskies love to charge the boat. That's why you gotta stay ready to reel in as fast as you can. Now I know you may get a huge backlash casting or reeling and that's another responsibility that Mason has. If you can't untangle a nasty bird's nest that'll be her job. Sorry, Mason."

Ray got a happy grin in return.

"All right, you razzbonyas. Get outta here. See you at five in the A.M. Doc, can you wait a minute? Need to talk to you."

"I am not worried about Mason if that's what you need to know," said Osborne as the two college boys climbed into their Toyota pickup and threw the little truck into a rapid reverse.

Watching them drive off, Ray shook his head. "Ah, those were the days. Seriously, Doc, I saw something out back of Buddy's Place that Chief Ferris needs to know about. She wasn't there when I had to leave so I told Bruce what I found but those two guys were so busy, I worry they'll forget to tell her. Is she staying at your place tonight? I'll walk over if she is. I took a photo of it."

"What are we talking about?" asked Osborne. "I'm not sure she'll be over tonight but I'll certainly be talking to her."

"Outside, back behind the trash bins, I found a deer cam up in a tree."

"Someone feeding deer illegally?"

"No. It was trained on that back entrance to the building. And it's wireless. Can't tell who it belongs to but somebody somewhere has been watching people coming and going back there. Strikes me as odd. Don't you think?"

"She told me you were finding plenty of footprints out there."

"Yeah, that ground is still soggy from the heavy rainfall we got two days ago. I got good shots of those. Bruce was happy with the photos, too. He thought the footprints outside looked like a match to the ones on that worktable and they are clear enough the guys in the crime lab should be able to tell what type of shoe including the brand and size.

"Let's just hope they aren't a Nike sneaker size twelve like every kid in America is wearing. So, yeah, Doc, I was able to track the footprints right up to where whoever it is got into a four-wheeler of some kind.

"But here's the confusing part: that deer cam was hung up far away from the footprints. I was looking so hard at the ground and the brush back there I almost missed the damn thing."

"Strange. And focused on the building?"

"Aimed right at that back door and, likely, the window beside it."

"So if we find the owner of the deer cam, we might be able to see who came and went last night?"

Ray nodded. "I feel bad I didn't take the time to remove it but there may be sign in the brush around the tree where it was hung that will help us find the owner. I took photos of the ground but I didn't have time to check the nearby brush for sign 'cause I had these boys showing up out here. On the other hand, since it's wireless, we can't do anything with it until we find the owner anyway."

"And that may take some time," said Osborne.

"Right, but still. I wish everything didn't always happen at once," said Ray shaking his head in frustration. "Please, tell Chief Ferris I'll be out there noon tomorrow while the boys are on break. I want to be sure she doesn't let anyone near the area until I can check it out."

"Is the area secured?" asked Osborne.

"Yes, Roger gave me a hand with that. Should be fine until I can get back out there."

Chapter Fourteen

Back at his house after watching Mason help Ray cover the gear on the picnic table with a large tarp and anchor it with rocks from the lake, Osborne made a decision that surprised even him: a decision that came straight from his heart. Inviting Mason into his den, he pulled over a chair so she could sit beside him. Before he sat down, he reached overhead for his prized muskie rod with its old but trustworthy Abu Garcia Ambassadeur Reel.

"When Ray gives you a little time off," said Osborne, "I want you to go ahead and see what you can do with this rod of mine. You're going to be hearing Ray instruct those boys, so you and I may as well take advantage of that. Don't you think?" He grinned at her. Mason looked stunned.

"It's my favorite muskie rod and it's got all new fishing line that I put on it this spring," he said, laying the rod across Mason's lap. "The line is hundred-pound test but you need to ask Ray if he can sell you one of those new leaders—the invisible ones. Tell him I'll pay for it."

"Grandpa, this is your best rod. Are you sure you want me—"

"I do and here's why. Being around Ray these next few days gives you a chance to learn a lot, too. But all the advice in the world doesn't help if you don't have good tools with which to practice.

So I want you to take this rod and reel and practice casting off the dock. When the tournament is over, I'll take you out in the boat. We'll go for one of those suspended mothers Ray keeps talking about. Sound good?"

"Can I use your surface mudpuppy, too?" Osborne was pleased to see that Mason's look of surprise had morphed into one of intense concentration.

"Don't you think that the Rizzo Tail might work better?"

"No, Grandpa, I know that mudpuppy is your favorite so I'd like to use that if you don't mind. I promise not to lose it." Osborne suppressed a grin. He didn't mention that Ralph's Sporting Goods kept a stash of surface mudpuppies just for him. He was notorious for losing way too many lures over the years.

Mason got to her feet and carefully set the rod and reel back up on the rack where Osborne kept it. "Gramps, I'm hungry. What's dinner?"

∽

After Osborne and Mason had polished off a couple of bratwursts that he found in the freezer along with some potato salad from the Loon Lake Market, Osborne's cell phone rang.

"Homicide," said Lew the second he answered. "No doubt about it, Doc. I'm still out here with Bruce and Rich. Bruce tried to get fingerprints off the downstairs lever that raises and lowers the piano but someone has wiped it clean. He could even tell the cleaning agent that was used. We figure that whoever went to all that trouble had to have been smart enough to wear gloves, too. Pretty slim likelihood the Wausau boys can get fingerprints worth anything."

"So Bruce is of the opinion there was a deliberate cleaning?"

"Yes and, Doc, he and I agree that while we may not have any concrete evidence to go on at this time common sense points to a double homicide. This was no accident."

"Based on what I saw out there, Lew, I agree," said Osborne. "One more—"

Before he could finish his sentence, Lew interrupted, saying, "Bruce is planning to dismantle the mechanism and send it to the lab. They have access to a new technology that can pick up prints even after a wipe-down but that'll take time.

"Funny, but no one is more surprised than Joyce Harmon. She was expecting her prints to be all over the damn lever."

"I'll bet she was but, say, Lew, before you get off the phone Ray wanted me to be sure to tell you that he found a wireless deer cam up in one of the trees out behind the building. He came across it just as he was leaving. He feels bad that he wasn't able to take more time exploring back there. He said you hadn't gotten back before he had to leave."

"No, I made the mistake of stopping by the department after we left Irene Niedermeier's. Bruce did mention something but he was so involved getting the piano lowered and those corpses examined and body-bagged, he didn't give me the details."

After Osborne filled her in on what Ray had told him, Lew was quiet. "Hmm, I wonder why anyone would do that? Maybe Chet thought he had someone stealing from the till after hours?"

"Ray said the deer cam is up in the tree if you want to check it out," said Osborne. "He and Roger taped off the area around the tree and nearby brush to be sure no one messes up any evidence of movement around there."

"No, I'll let that wait until morning. We might miss something in the dark. But I called to see if you can meet me in my office first thing tomorrow? I've arranged for our three fraud victims—

you know the upstanding citizens I'm referring to—to meet us at nine. I would love for you to sit in on that interrogation. I believe it behooves having a man hear what they have to say."

"Of course I will be there. Mason will be busy helping Ray and his fishing team so I don't have to worry about her. Plus I wouldn't miss it for the world.

"Lewellyn, why is your life so much more interesting than mine?"

She chuckled. "I doubt you would feel that way if you saw the paperwork I have yet to tackle tonight. Oh, and I'm hoping we can meet with the woman who has been working with Tiffany. Nina Krezminski is her name. Roger and I have been calling her cell number but no answer, yet. I hope to schedule her interrogation right after the men's."

The next morning Osborne didn't have a chance to wake Mason, who was sleeping in the downstairs bedroom that had been her mother's when she was growing up. The smartphone she'd been given for her birthday had an alarm feature, which she must have used because it was four fifteen A.M. when Mike jumped off his dog bed and ran, tail wagging, to the kitchen.

"Oh, hi, Gramps. I didn't want to wake you up." She was in the midst of plunging a spoon into a bowl of dry cereal. A glass of orange juice and a peeled banana indicated she had her breakfast well under control. "You can go back to bed," she said with a gentle smile.

"No," said Osborne, "I'll pull on my clothes and walk you over."

Within five minutes, Mason was ready to go.

"And you have your phone, right, young lady? Your mother insists you keep that phone with you every minute."

Mason patted the left back pocket of her jean shorts. "Right here, Grandpa. I got my backpack, too." She held up a bright blue backpack. "Got my new waders and my hat in here."

And with that they walked out the back door, across the yard to the driveway, and through a stand of balsams (one of Osborne's late wife's failed efforts to hide the presence of Ray's trailer home from her guests). After ducking through branches, Osborne tried to keep up with Mason as she ran down the two-lane dirt drive to Ray's.

"Hey, look, I'm the first one here." Standing in the clearing in front of the neon green muskie, the clearing empty except for Ray's battered blue pickup, she beamed up at her grandfather, her eyes sparkling in the faint haze of the early morning sun.

Ray opened his screen door and beckoned her inside. With a quick wave to Osborne, she disappeared.

It was just after seven when he finished his coffee at McDonald's and, having dodged too many questions about the peculiarities he had witnessed at Buddy's Place, Osborne decided to head over to Lew's office to see if she might be in early.

His hunch was right. She was at her desk, eyes focused on her computer screen and fingers moving rapidly. "Morning, Doc. Grab a cup of coffee," she said without looking up. "Almost finished here." A ring on her desk phone forced her to stop what she was doing and answer.

"Yes, Joyce, what is it? You are kidding. How long ago? Yes, please, give me the address." Lew scribbled something on one of the sticky notes she kept by the phone. "I'll check it out right now." Setting the phone down, she got to her feet. "Grab one of those paper cups and bring your coffee with you, Doc. Joyce said that woman is skipping town."

"What woman?"

"Nina Krezminski, Tiffany Niedermeier's sidekick. She was just at the club. She tried to make Joyce open up so she could grab some clothes and makeup. Joyce refused. Told her the club is off-limits by order of law enforcement. Then this Nina person let go with enough expletives that Joyce doesn't trust her."

Within ten minutes, Lew's cruiser was turning down a sloping drive toward a shabby apartment building built years ago to resemble a Swiss chalet. If it resembled anything today, it was not Swiss and not a chalet but a wood frame structure with doors in need of paint and sagging, weed-filled window boxes. One of the doors stood open as a woman in jeans and a blue-striped T-shirt hurried out with a box she shoved into the trunk of an older model Honda Civic.

"Nina Krezminski?" Lew called as she got out of the cruiser.

The woman stopped and stared, shoulders sagging. "Why?"

"Chief Lewellyn Ferris of the Loon Lake Police," said Lew, walking toward her. "I thought we had a meeting later this morning."

"So? I'll be there."

"Looks to me like you're going somewhere."

"I have a job interview this afternoon. Going back to the cities."

"Not until we talk you aren't. If you try to leave I'll put you under arrest for leaving the scene of a crime."

"You can't do that!"

"Where were you Tuesday night?"

"Working at Buddy's Place until one in the morning like I was supposed to. Then I came home."

"That's what *you* say. I have no reason to believe that. Is there someone who can vouch they saw you there that late?"

A stupefied expression crossed the woman's face. She looked all around her as if she might find a better answer in the parking lot.

Meanwhile Osborne got out of the cruiser but stood next to it waiting in case Lew wanted him to block the car. He wasn't sure that would be a good idea but he was game.

"If you're in such a rush, why don't we talk now?"

"Here?"

"Back in your apartment. Dr. Osborne is one of my deputies and I'll have him make a quick call to let dispatch know we'll be a few minutes late for my nine o'clock. Doc, will you bring that tape recorder that's on the back seat, please?"

"Well, look at this," said Lew, walking through the front room of the small apartment, which appeared to be furnished by the building's owners. "You do have everything packed up, don't you?"

Without waiting for an answer, Lew pulled out a small wooden chair fronting a table large enough for two. "If you'll sit across from me, Ms. Krezminski, this will work fine."

While she set up the tape recorder, Osborne pulled an armchair close enough to the table so any comment or question he might make would register on the tape recorder. Then he took a minute to look around.

A sofa bed messy with sheets and blankets anchored the opposite wall and across from them was a small kitchenette. The apartment reeked of cigarette smoke so badly that Osborne walked over to crack open a window.

Nina Krezminski was a bird-boned woman with reddish-blonde bangs nearly covering her eyes. Her face, overtanned and heavily freckled, reminded Osborne of a wizened monkey. As Osborne returned to his chair, she dropped her head to look up at him from below the bangs. It was a coy, entreating look from eyes fringed with lashes so thick he wondered if Nina could see through them. Later Lew would assure him the lashes were fake.

"Until yesterday, you have been working with Tiffany Niedermeier at Buddy's Place on the north end of the town of Loon Lake, correct?"

"Yes." Her voice, tinged with a Southern drawl, was redolent of cigarettes, Scotch whiskey, and late nights.

"You both worked for Chet Wright, the owner, correct?"

"Yes."

"Please describe for me the nature of your work for Mr. Wright."

"We . . . um . . . assisted the customers. We provided drinks and . . . um . . . entertainment."

"So you bartended and danced?"

"I bartended, well kind of. I served drinks. Tiffany danced. I don't dance."

"What were your wages?"

The woman hesitated. She dropped her eyes and peered through her bangs. "Twenty-five an hour."

"Ms. Krezminski," said Lew in an even tone, "I suggest you drop the innocent routine and give me honest answers. I happen to know that whatever the club reported to the IRS, you could in fact make fifteen hundred a night. Am I not correct?"

There was a long pause while Nina looked Lew up and down. "If I say yes, should I assume next you'll want *pictures*?" The Southern accent was gone, voice snide.

"No, your clients plan to show me those," said Lew. "I don't need details either. But what I do want to know is how the credit card scheme worked. What was your role in that? What was Tiffany's? What did Chet—"

"Okay, okay." Nina started to sob, though her heaving sounded fake to Osborne. "I had to do it. I had to. I had to. She m-m-ade me."

"Who made you do what? Tiffany?" Nina continued to make the annoying sounds.

"Come on now, let's cut the baloney. Nina, if you will cooperate with this investigation, I'm sure we can work out something to keep you out of jail but I need to know you are telling the truth. Right now I don't believe a word you're saying. Want to start over?"

Nina took a deep breath, then spoke in a voice hard and clear. "Here's the truth. I met Tiffany last summer in a club in Minneapolis where she was dancing. Chet Wright came in often. He had a thing for her. They talked me into coming here to help with the new place and I thought it might be a good way to start over, y'know.

"And I kind of had to, see. Tiffany knew I'd had a little dustup with some boys running coke a couple years back. She threatened to tell them where I was if I didn't help her. I couldn't let that happen—they might kill me. Beat me up for sure and you know . . ."

Lew nodded in sympathy. "I can only imagine. I can see you had no choice."

"Then she stole from me, too. Yes, I got paid fifteen hundred but I had to give her half, which is not fair. She took stuff from me, too. My good jewelry, a new sweater. That bitch just helped herself. But thing is—what I want you to know—is all I ever did was get those boys real drunk . . ."

"You mean the men from Deer Creek who patronized Buddy's Place?"

"Yeah. All I did was get them drunk and stoned enough that me and Tiffany could take pictures that looked like they did more than they ever did. Frankly, they weren't capable of doing anything.

"Then Chet would drive 'em over to where they were staying and roll 'em into bed. He's the one who ran the charges for drinks and entertainment. I never touched a credit card machine. Never, I swear.

"Later he and Tiffany would fool around at the club. On that piano and stuff. But, see, thing is Tiffany was mean as hell. You want to know who all might want to kill her? It's a long list.

"Start with old Joyce. It wasn't just the way Tiffany talked to her. Tiff left filth all over the place that Joyce had to clean up. Joyce could do it, too, see."

"What do you mean?" asked Lew. "Joyce could clean up?"

"No, no, she could be the killer." The coy look. "She knows how to run that piano up and down. I think she's the one got those two crushed to death."

"How do you know about the piano and what's happened?"

"Everyone in Loon Lake knows. I heard yesterday afternoon."

"She's right, Chief," said Osborne. "I got quizzed by the boys at McDonald's this morning. It may not be on TV but it's all over town."

"Let's go back for a minute, Nina," said Lew. "What makes you so sure Joyce could be involved?"

"Two things," said Nina. "First, she kept that piano so well oiled it barely made noise when it was raised and lowered. Then you have that antique jukebox goin' full blast. Trust me, Tiffany and Chet wouldn't have heard anything if they were . . . you know, *not paying attention*, shall we say." The coy look again. This time with a glint of malice.

"I didn't notice the jukebox," said Lew.

"You didn't? It's over in the corner. Probably turned off when you were there, otherwise all the lights are on so you can't miss it. Chet paid a fortune to have it restored. The jukebox and the piano, those were his toys. He was very proud of how well they worked."

"Who else hated Tiffany? Besides you and Joyce?" Nina threw Lew a quick look like she was going to argue but thought better of it.

"God, how many fingers do you have? Most are people over in the cities. 'Course, then there's squinty little Fred. Tiffany loved making fun of him, too. At first I think he had a crush on her. You know, Tiffany was not a bad-looking woman and she has a body that never stops so you can't blame a guy.

"Here's a good example of how wonderful Tiffany could be. One day right after Fred did something nice like let her borrow his golf cart to go for a ride around the preserve, she says to him in front of all of us, 'Hey, Fred, anyone ever tell you you're concrete up to your neck and shit the rest of the way?' Then she laughed so hard.

"I thought the poor guy was going to cry. And there was no reason for her to say that. He never did nothing bad to her." Nina shook her head, remembering.

"You had good reason to hate her," said Lew in an understanding tone of voice.

"I did. I surely did. But I didn't kill her if that's what you think."

"Do you feel bad she's gone?"

Nina's eyes swung from Lew to Osborne. No longer coy, the expression in them was flat: flat and dead. She didn't answer.

"The good news, Nina," said Lew, "is I believe you; the bad news is you cannot leave Loon Lake until I say you can."

"Guess I sorta figured that. Okay. I'll stay here though if that's all right."

"Yes. I'm interrogating the gentlemen from the Deer Creek Preserve this morning and I may have more questions for you after that session."

Nina snorted. "*Gentlemen?*" Her monkey face gave a sardonic grin.

"Lewellyn," said Osborne, hitting the button to lower the passenger side window in the cruiser, "hope this isn't too much wind. I need fresh air."

"Me, too," said Lew and put her window down. "What do you think, Doc?"

"Nina? I think she feels trapped. Tiffany stealing from her, probably putting her down in front of the customers, threatening to expose her to the drug dealers if she didn't do what she was told.

"Wouldn't surprise me if she tried to sabotage Tiffany in some way. Now she worries we'll find out and wonder if she isn't the one who pulled the lever. Yep, that's why she's so quick to place the blame on someone else. What else would you do if you felt the facts closing in on you?"

"Same thing an animal does," said Lew. "You fight your way out.

"Doc, that woman had no intention of showing up for the interrogation. I'll have Dani run a criminal background check and I'll bet you anything we'll find Nina Krezminski's run out on more than that. If that is her real name."

Chapter Fifteen

Lew's office felt cramped and stuffy when Osborne walked in behind her. Three men sat waiting in chairs under the windows. Two wore tan dress pants and button-down shirts open at the collar.

The third man, corpulent, was dressed in a faded gray pullover that hung loose over a pair of wrinkled black shorts in serious need of a washing machine. Bulbous knees and battered flip-flops completed a picture Osborne saw too often during the tourist season.

All except the fat man stood when Lew walked into the room. Introducing herself and Osborne, she said, "Gentlemen, thank you for coming in this morning, and I apologize if we are a few minutes late. I am Lewellyn Ferris, chief of the Loon Lake Police." She gestured toward Osborne as he pulled a chair closer to where the men were sitting.

"Dr. Paul Osborne here is one of my deputies. He often assists my department and the Wausau Crime Lab as an odontologist. As you might imagine it is very helpful to have an expert in dental forensics standing by when we need him. Dr. Osborne also assists with other elements of investigations since I have only two full-time officers to help with law enforcement here in Loon Lake."

"Ya got the sheriff's department, don't ya," said black shorts, still sitting with one chubby leg crossed over the other, his left foot bouncing.

"They have the county to cover, Mr. . . . ?"

"Bronk, Bert Bronk. Oak Park, Illinois. My old man owned every Walgreens north of Chicago and all the way to goddamn North Pole. Been coming to Deer Creek since I was born and I never saw a Loon Lake cop ever." He gave a laugh that ended with a loud hacking. Too many cigars, thought Osborne as the sound from the man's throat turned his stomach.

"Well, that surprises me," said Lew calmly. "The Loon Lake Police Department has been in existence at least seventy-five years. Our jurisdiction is the Loon Lake Township, which is why you're here this morning. Buddy's Place is located just inside the township line—"

"The Deer Creek Preserve sure as hell isn't. It's in the next county," barked black shorts.

"True." Osborne thought Lew was remaining remarkably genial in light of the man's borderline rudeness. "The crimes we are here to discuss happened in Loon Lake so—"

"I got nothin' to say about that. These fellas don't either so let's just wind this up. We all got business to do."

"Certainly. Please follow me down to our conference room."

As if to distance themselves from their heavy-set compatriot, the other two men who had been standing in silence now extended their hands to Lew first and then to Osborne.

"Good morning," said the man closest to Lew, "I'm Jud Westerman, also from Chicago. Retired commodities trader and my great-grandfather was one of the founders of Deer Creek." A tall hawk-faced man, Westerman had a booming voice and a shock of white hair over a well-tanned face.

"Haven't I seen you on the golf course over in Rhinelander?" asked Osborne as he shook his hand.

"Wouldn't be surprised. I'm there three mornings a week when I'm up north. That is one premier golf course you folks got there."

"And I'm Pete Kretzler," said the third man, giving Osborne's hand an extra squeeze: a silent signal. "Hand surgeon from Milwaukee. It's my wife's family has the membership. We just built a lake home in Minocqua for when I retire. Chief Ferris, Dr. Osborne, certainly happy to help out any way I can."

Jowly with a wide, full mouth and a big head, Kretzler had a nose that threatened to take over his face unless he cut back on the whiskey. Osborne nodded as he shook the man's hand and looked briefly into his eyes. He had seen Kretzler several times in the room behind the glass door with the coffeepot on it: the AA meeting place. But that was confidential and to be shared with no one, not even the Loon Lake chief of police.

Once in the conference room, Lew directed the men to sit in specific chairs then pointed to the young woman standing at the back of the room.

"Dani, our intern back there, is also our IT guru. She'll be helping us this morning. Like Dr. Osborne and myself, she knows to keep everything said in this room confidential." The three men glanced quickly at Dani and the video camera.

"Dani," asked Lew, "are we ready to videotape this session?"

"Yes, Chief, but let me give you and Dr. Osborne some directions on how to operate the equipment in case I have to leave."

Dani motioned for them to join her out in the hallway. Closing the door softly behind her, Dani whispered, "I did what you asked. Got two extra video setups from the sheriff's department and now I'll adjust the cameras so you get full face on each of the men. I think I should stay in case they move around, turn away, whatever. I'll be in the back where they probably won't notice me. Does that work for you?"

"That will be very helpful," said Lew. "Are we ready to start then?"

"Yes."

After Lew described the scene she had come upon at the club, she told the three that she was aware that they had been patronizing the club and alleged they had had bogus charges applied to their credit cards.

"Am I correct in the details so far?" she asked after describing what she had learned from Ty Wallis.

"Oh yeah. The total on mine might even be more than a hundred sixty grand," said Bert Bronk, hocking another wad of phlegm as he tried to adjust his shorts. "Got my office manager checking with my bank today. We think more charges went in over the weekend."

"I assume you three know that I know about the alleged compromising positions in which you were photographed. Depending on what transpires during our investigation, I may need you to share some of those photos." All three men studied the floor.

Pete, the hand surgeon, was the first to respond. "Can you do that in a way that I don't have to tell my wife? I . . . it would not be good for my marriage."

Osborne was not surprised to hear that. During the few AA meetings he had attended, Pete had admitted that his drinking was threatening his marriage, not to mention his career in medicine. Pete was struggling and Osborne felt for him.

He remembered his own dark days and said a quick prayer of thanks for his life today. He stole a glance at Lew. But for his closest friends—Lew, Ray Pradt, and the support of his daughters who forced an intervention—he might be just another whiskey-sodden drunk like Pete.

"Won't help mine either," said Jud, referring to his marriage.

"Hell, I don't care what the hell you do. Just find who killed that idiot Wright so we can put this behind us. Goddammit," said Bronk. "For the record, Chief Ferris, I did not solicit any females—I was solicited. Got that? *Solicited.* No crime in listening is there?"

"I am not here to serve warrants for soliciting prostitutes or for hiding credit card fraud," said Lew. "I am conducting a homicide investigation."

"Oh, for Chrissake, you keep saying 'homicide,'" said Bronk. "What makes you think it wasn't just some dumb accident? Chet was all excited and he hit the damn lever with his foot. That's what I think." Bronk thrust his chin into the air with the air of a man used to giving orders.

"Mr. Bronk, I hear you but I assure you that we have found evidence, which information I am not at liberty to share at this time, that a double homicide did take place."

Lew gave Bert a long, level look. "I'm hoping one of you or all of you might help us generate a lead on who might have wanted Chet Wright dead."

"That's a tough one," said Jud. "Chet may have been irritating at times but he was a pretty entertaining fellow. Easy to have a good time with the guy." Jud looked at each of his friends. "You agree Bert, Pete?"

"Yeah, he was fun," said Pete ruefully. "Maybe not the best kind of fun . . . obviously."

"Now, gentlemen," said Lew as she opened a manila file on the table in front of her, "there is good reason to cooperate by sharing everything you may know about the goings on at Buddy's Place. You do realize you did not do yourselves any favors by trying to sweep the credit card fraud under the carpet and not alerting authorities. Under the circumstances you might be considered accessories to the crime."

Lew sat back and waited. Osborne kept quiet.

"Yeah, I just want my money back," said Bronk. He leaned forward. "Every goddamn penny. You tell Wright's widow that. He might be dead but *she* owes me."

"Karen Wright may have to declare bankruptcy," said Osborne. "Chet appears to have gambled away all their assets. Even Buddy's Place is mortgaged."

"Oh yeah?" Bronk leaned back, looking even fatter as he did so. "Then you tell me what the hell she's going to do when she gets that five-million-dollar payout on Chet's life insurance. You tell me that."

"How do you know there's life insurance?" asked Lew.

The other two men looked on in surprise. This was news to them.

"Chet told me. Two years ago she made him take it out before she would give the okay for him to sit at the baccarat table in Vegas. If he didn't take it out, she was going to divorce him, which at that time would have been a financial disaster for the guy.

"See," Bert wriggled in his chair before saying, "Chet's problem was he liked to think he wore the big pants. Y'know what I mean? But he could never shake off that wife of his. She ran the show.

"So trust me. I know there's five million buckaroos sitting out there and she does too." As he spoke, Pete Kretzler picked at an invisible spot on his slacks. Osborne, watching him, wondered what the man was thinking.

Fifteen minutes later, as the men were about to leave, Osborne said, "Chief Ferris, I'll be back in half an hour. I need to drive home and check on my granddaughter."

But that was not where he went first. After hurrying to the parking lot, he watched Pete climb into a black BMW and head out on County C in the direction of the Wright mansion. Osborne stayed a discreet distance behind Pete's car, pleased for once that he drove a light-colored Subaru that looked like a hundred others on the streets of Loon Lake.

The BMW turned off at Tall Timbers Drive and drove east half a mile before taking another right into the circular drive that swept up to the Wright residence. Osborne drove past two houses then turned around as quick as he could. He pulled over across the street, a few hundred feet from the Wright driveway.

Through a screen of arbor vitae, he watched as Pete stood waiting before the massive front doors to the mansion. He must have rung the doorbell twice because he stood there for a minute or two before one of the doors swung open and Karen stepped out. Pete opened his arms wide and she folded herself into his embrace. Then she pulled him by the arm into the house.

Osborne put his car in gear and drove home to check on Mason.

Chapter Sixteen

Mason scarfed down her wild rice soup and two peanut butter sandwiches so fast Osborne worried she might choke to death. Between sandwich bites, she gave a breathless update: "Yeah, Gramps, the boys got two small muskies this morning but not big enough to qualify. Ray's not worried. He said tonight's fishing will be better—something about the moon, I'm not sure.

"But the good news is he told me while they're gone, I can use his fishing kayak. Have you seen that, Gramps? It is so cool."

"Honey, slow down and eat your lunch. I'm afraid you're going to choke on that peanut butter." He resisted the urge to remind her to chew with her mouth closed.

"No, no, I'm fine. So anyway, I'm gonna go for that Buster—you know that big muskie Ray said hides in the reeds out in front of his dock?"

"Yes, I do," said Osborne absent-mindedly. Now that it appeared Mason would survive lunch he was thinking back to the events of the morning.

"Gramps," said Mason, "you aren't listening."

"Yes, yes, I am."

He was trying to listen but the image of Pete Kretzler embracing Karen Wright bothered him. Was it a hug of sympathy or something else? As soon as Mason was finished with her lunch, he would call Lew.

". . . so my plan is to keep calling her Buster. Real loud. She's a girl, right? What girl wants to be called Buster? If I make her mad, maybe she'll come at me. Like Ray says—the big ones like to charge the boat. So if she comes at me, then maybe I can catch her 'cause I got your rod and reel. So I'll keep going 'Buster, Buster, Buster.'" She swung her spoon in the air and Osborne ducked the flying soup.

"Mason, sweetheart, please stop jumping up and down on your chair. Now, what are you doing this afternoon because I have to go back to town to help Chief Ferris? I'll be back by five and we'll have an early supper."

"Ray gave me a list of lures and other stuff he wants me to clean and put away while he and the boys are out fishing. You don't need to make me dinner, Gramps. Ray said he's got some fresh walleye he's going to sauté up for us with little red potatoes."

"No, honey," said Osborne, "I was going to bake that chicken recipe you love . . ." The look on Mason's face told Osborne his special chicken was not her meal of choice. Or was it that she preferred the company of one tall, bearded fishing guide and two college boys? Silly me, thought her grandfather. He knew the answer to that.

"Oh say, Gramps, I almost forgot. Ray wants you to give him a call. Like right away."

"Oh?" Osborne shoved his chair back and reached for the cordless phone hanging on his kitchen wall. He punched in the number for Ray's cell. "Mason, honey, I wish you'd told me earlier," he was saying as Ray answered.

"Yo, Doc," said Ray, "I'm out here at Buddy's Place for the next half hour or so. I got that deer cam down from the tree and been checking for more sign between the club and the preserve but haven't found anything. Not sure what to do about this wireless deer cam. Like how to find the owner?"

"Have you talked to Lew about it?"

"Not yet. They said she'd call me later. I'll be heading back to my place in a few minutes so how 'bout I drop it off and let you take it in?"

"Fine. Lew's expecting me so that works."

"How's Mason doing? We kept her busy this morning. Is she okay with everything?"

"Seems pretty darn happy to me. I could barely get her to settle down and eat lunch. She said you're okay with her using a kayak? I didn't know you have one."

"It's a loaner. One of these CarbonLite boats, a new model this company wants me to test for fishing. She can't hurt the darn thing, Doc, and I can see she's dying to go after Buster." Ray laughed. "Be amazing if she gets a rise from that fish."

"Jeez, I hope not. That would scare her to death. Now, Ray, is the kayak safe for an eleven-year-old?"

"She can swim, can't she?"

"Yes, but—"

"She'll be fine. I'll make sure she takes a life jacket if she goes. Hold on a minute, Doc, Bruce is texting me."

Seconds later, Ray said, "He said to ask you and Chief Ferris if you got time for some fly-fishing tonight. He has to be back in Wausau in the morning and he figures to finish up here at Buddy's Place by dinnertime."

"Tell him I'll check with Lew and get back to him."

"Okay and, Doc, I'll be sure Mason's home by nine."

Osborne washed the lunch dishes, fed the dog, and corralled Mason to walk down to the dock with him for his usual noontime check of baby ducklings. Minus two. Hmm, the muskies were feeding. Mason was stricken at the thought of the two babies eaten by the shark of the north. "I know, hon," said her grandfather, "but it's nature's way. Nothing we can do about it."

He was back up in the kitchen just in time to see Ray's pickup pull into Osborne's driveway. Ray hopped out, put a box holding the deer cam on the back seat of Osborne's car, and gave a wave toward the kitchen window as he drove off.

"Mason?" Osborne called after his granddaughter as he headed out the back door to his car, "I'm heading back to town to work with Chief Ferris. Now don't forget to take your phone with you today. Have you got it?" He paused, waiting for a response. "Mason? Did you hear me?"

"Yes, Grandpa. I never forget," she called back. "Don't you forget yours either."

"Got it," said Osborne. "Thanks for the reminder." He smiled, patting Mike on the head as he walked by. "Take good care of her, fella."

Osborne laid the deer cam on Lew's desk. She stared at it. "I have no idea how to find out who owns or runs this thing . . ." She picked up her phone and hit the number for Dani's extension. "I'm putting her on speaker, Doc.

"Question, Dani. I have a deer cam here that's wireless. Ray found it up in a tree out at the crime scene at Buddy's Place. Do you think there's a way we can find out who the owner is? Even if it's just Chet Wright, I need to know."

"Should be easy," said Dani. "I'll be right over to your office with my laptop."

Five minutes after walking in, she was able to access the deer cam's hard drive through information provided by the manufacturer. It was registered to an owner whose e-mail started with *jharmon*.

"That is as much as I can find," said Dani. "I need the owner's security code to access the video itself," she said.

Lew looked over at Osborne, who was watching over Dani's shoulder. "That has to be Joyce Harmon. Let's go, Doc. Why on earth would she be watching people coming and going through the back door of Buddy's Place?"

"I was watching me."

"I don't understand," said Lew with a quick glance at Osborne. They'd found Joyce looking as unkempt as ever and busy mopping the floor in the dining room kitchen of the preserve.

"Sorry, Joyce, but would you put that mop down for a minute? Dr. Osborne and I need to talk to you." Lew pointed her to the empty dining room where she had set the deer cam on the table.

Startled at the sight of the unit, Joyce had said, "This has nothing to do with what happened at the club if that's what you're thinking."

"I don't know what to think until you tell us why you put this camera up in the tree."

Joyce looked so miserable Osborne felt sorry for her. "Does this have something to do with critters like squirrels or raccoons getting into the club?" he asked, hoping he was right.

"Nah. It's just me." Joyce laced her fingers together and set her hands on the table, shoulders slumping, as if she was about to confess a terrible crime. "Fred hates me. He wants Mr. Wallis to fire me. He says I'm a mess even if I do everything I'm s'posed to. I think he's OCD, but I don't tell him that. Seriously, I'm the one keeps everything spic and span and all he can do is unplug a goddamn toilet. But I was late one day—just one day—and ever since then he's been accusing me of not getting here on time."

"I heard him question you on that yesterday morning," said Lew.

"See, thing is Mr. Wallis hired me before he hired Fred. And . . ." She paused before saying more. "Well, thing is he hired me in spite of the fact I have a felony on my record."

"A felony? That's serious," said Lew. "What kind of felony?"

"Ten years ago, I took some money from a convenience store where I was a clerk. I shouldna done it. I paid it back but with that on my record," Joyce raised sad eyes, "I can't get a job. If I lose this job . . .

"I come to work through that back door, so I put up the deer cam to prove to Fred that I am on time. Every day, I am on time or early. Sounds crazy but it's the only way I can protect myself 'cause I'm the only person here in the morning."

"Joyce," said Osborne, "was this camera operating Monday night?"

He threw a quick look at Lew. "Because you might have video of whoever it was that came in that night. Have you watched it recently?"

"No. I've only watched it once to be sure it was working. I figure it's something I can make Fred watch next time he tries to say I was late."

"Okay, Joyce. How do we watch it?" asked Lew with excitement in her voice. "Can we plug it in here somewhere?"

"No. You have to watch at my house on this laptop I got," said Joyce. "I guess you want to go there?"

Joyce lived in a small wood frame house tucked behind the paper mill. While Lew paced back and forth in the tiny living room, Joyce set the receiver for the deer cam on her kitchen table. "Okay, it's on," she said. "Since it's motion-activated something should come up right away."

She was right but the first images were disappointing: Ray Pradt. Once they got past the video of Ray discovering and staring into the deer cam, they waited. A digital date and time in one corner of the screen came on: four A.M. on Tuesday morning.

The camera was focused on the door with a corner of the window visible. As they watched, in the far right corner of the screen was a figure in dark clothing that appeared to be approaching the window at the back of the club. Over the next few minutes, all they could make out was the figure entering the open window, then backing out and disappearing off to the right. Whoever it was never faced the camera.

Lew had Joyce run the sequence back and forth half a dozen times before giving up. "So we got something but not enough," she said, muttering to herself.

"Okay, I want Bruce to see this. Maybe the Wausau boys can figure out height or some other distinguishing characteristics here. Maybe they've got a way to clarify the image. They do wonders with security cameras these days. Even if all they can tell us is whether or not that figure is a man or a woman—that would help.

"Joyce, I need to take your deer cam, your laptop, and the receiver with us. And I need your security code. Sorry about that, but this is evidence from the crime scene."

"Go right ahead," said Joyce.

"I have a question, Joyce," said Osborne while helping Lew pack up the equipment. "Why is Fred so set on firing you? Is it something you did here? Maybe this isn't a fair question, but I don't understand."

"I haven't done anything, except you know how really well dressed he is? I bet you he irons his underpants. He tells me all the time I'm a slob. I think he wants someone kind of perfect like him. But, for Chrissake, I move garbage and trash all day. I clean toilets, I—plus he's just weird. What can I say? Sometimes people just don't like you and vice versa. I got an uncle I can't be around, y'know. I know Fred does everything Mr. Wallis needs him to do, but I'm not going to let him ruin my life."

A glint entered her eye. "I'll tell you something though. Much as he hates *me*, that Tiffany couldn't stand *him*. She gave him a hard time even though he made me do lots of extra stuff for her."

"Like what extra stuff?" asked Lew.

"Clean towels, clean her rooms at the lodge, which I am not supposed to do. Fix snacks and candies for her dressing table. She was such a pig, too. Dirty Kleenex, used condoms, I always had to clean up after her in ways I shouldn't have to. Nina doesn't leave crap around like that. Mr. Wright was pretty decent, too."

"What about Karen Wright?" asked Lew.

"What about her?"

"Was she ever at Buddy's Place?"

"Oh sure, lots of times. She's been working on something with Fred. Not sure what but she comes by in that golf cart of his and they go somewhere. I have no idea where. Hey, are those two brother and sister?"

"What makes you say that?" asked Osborne, taken aback.

"They're so nice to each other. Like they take care of each other. I dunno, maybe I'm wrong."

"Didn't Karen mention they grew up next door to each other?" asked Lew.

"That's right. I forgot about that," said Osborne.

"Whatever," said Joyce with a shrug. "She treats him like he's her baby brother."

Chapter Seventeen

"Was there anyone to whom Tiffany was not unpleasant?" asked Osborne as they walked into Lew's office, where Bruce was waiting for them in one of the chairs in front of Lew's desk.

"I assume that's a rhetorical question, Doc," said Lew, sitting down at her desk and reaching for the files that Bruce was handing to her.

She had started to look at the documents when Bruce distracted her, saying in a petulant voice, "Hey, people, about time you got here. How are we going to get work done and still have time with the fly rod if you don't move it and shake it?"

"Oh-h-h, I forgot," said Osborne. "You two will have to go yourselves. I need to get back for Mason."

"You do?" Lew gave him a look of surprise. "I thought you told me she works for Ray until nine or something like that."

"That's true," said Osborne. "And she did tell me Ray was sautéing walleye for her and the boys tonight. So, yeah, I guess I can go."

"Excellent," said Bruce with a leap of his eyebrows.

"So we have cause of death, do we?" asked Lew, looking up from one document she was holding.

"Yes. Asphyxiation. Both victims. They were crushed up against that twelve-foot-high ceiling. The autopsy tests showed levels of intoxication so high we doubt they heard a thing as that motorized piano hoist raised the two of them up. Drug tests aren't back yet but I won't be surprised if we don't have evidence of controlled substances too."

"Great. This data is official, Doc. You can enter it on the death certificates. What about those footprints, Bruce. Any news on those?" asked Lew.

"Yes, indeed. Vasque hiking boots, men's size ten. Sold at Ralph's Sporting Goods, Cabela's, and Fleet Farm. A little too popular if you ask me. Might be tough to find the right pair as plenty of serious outdoors folk buy those."

"Hey, it's a start," said Lew. "Better than nothing. Answers one question anyway. If it's a man's boot then we have to be looking for a male suspect. Wouldn't you say?"

"True, and the boots do have a very visible wear pattern, so if you have a suspect and that suspect owns Vasque hiking boots, the guys at the lab will have a good shot at matching the boots to the prints left on the workbench. Boots don't match? You might have the wrong guy. How's that for a day's work?"

Bruce jumped up from his chair. "Let's go throw a few lines, hey."

"Not so fast," said Lew, motioning for him to take his seat again. "We found the owner of that wireless deer cam that was hung up in a tree back by those garbage bins. Doc, will you please unpack the units? Let's put them on the table over by the windows."

Carrying the cardboard box holding Joyce's deer cam and its receiver, Osborne set the devices on the table and moved out of the way so Bruce could examine them.

"Whoa, a GSM Drone Remote Surveillance System, cool," said Bruce, hovering over the table. "I've been planning to check out one of those for deer hunting. But, man, they are expensive. I know you can upload the images to your phone but, jeez, do you really need that much hi-tech baloney out in the woods?"

"Joyce Harmon did. She figured five hundred bucks was worth it to save her job," said Lew. The three of them gathered around the low table.

"Sit tight, Bruce. I want you to view what Doc and I saw and see what you think. Doc, will you turn the receiver on, please?"

Osborne and Lew watched over Bruce's shoulder as the image of the dark figure approaching the window appeared on the small screen.

"Can you run that again?" asked Bruce, leaning forward and intent on the small screen. "Hard to make out much, isn't it? Frankly, looks like a bear climbing in that window."

"Yeah, tough to see," said Lew. "Whoever it is never turns around so we can get a good look at the face."

Bruce was quiet, saying nothing as he had Osborne run the video two more times. "Tell you what," he said finally. "Let me share this with one of my guys in the lab. We might be able to get height and weight detail, which could help once you have a suspect."

"I was hoping you might say that," said Lew.

"But first," said Bruce, taking over from Osborne, "let me try to e-mail this video down to the lab . . . there . . . good . . . looks like it sent fine." He sat back saying, "Tomorrow morning before I leave town, I'll stop back at Buddy's Place and take some measurements out back there. That should make it easy for us to get an accurate profile of that figure.

"Can we go fishing now?"

"Bruce, Doc and I need an hour to finish up here," said Lew. "Hold your horses, will you?"

"All right," said Bruce grudgingly, "I'll go pack my things. Call me when you're ready."

As it was, Lew didn't finish up with her paperwork and phone calls until after seven. About the same time, Osborne was able to complete most of the information required for the death certificates. "I'm starving," said Lew.

"Me, too," said Osborne.

They met up with Bruce at the Loon Lake Pub for burgers and fries. Bruce compounded their unhealthy menu with a large order of cheese curds.

When everyone was satisfied, Lew said, "We'll do the Surprise tonight. I haven't fished that stream since last fall, plus it isn't too far away. Bruce, you'll have to follow us. We'll park and walk in about half a mile."

The drive took less than twenty minutes. They pulled into a clearing and unpacked their gear. Once everyone had their waders on and rods ready, Osborne and Bruce followed behind Lew as she tromped through a landscape of tamarack, tag alder, swamp grass, balsam, birch, and red pine.

The going wasn't difficult, though Osborne had to duck a number of times to protect his fly rod and avoid tearing a hole in his waders. Twice Lew stopped to check her compass and be sure they weren't lost. "Hey, it's worth it." She grinned back at Bruce and Osborne. "We'll find native brook trout back here. Can't beat it."

"OMG, it's a caddisfly hatch," cried Bruce as they emerged out of the woods onto the bank of a small stream. "Man oh man, it's a feeding frenzy." He dropped to his knees, fingers fumbling at a small plastic container of trout flies. "What do you say, Chief? An Adams?"

"No," said Lew, "here. Tie this on—it's a Deep Sparkle Pupa, size twelve." She handed him a small brown trout fly and turned to Osborne. "Doc, here's a Deep Sparkle for you. This one is green.

"Now, Bruce, I want you to cast that fly out and let it sink to the bottom, then draw it in slowly, very slowly." She stood on the bank of the small stream to watch Bruce.

Osborne was still busy tying on his fly when Lew gave a loud yelp. "Bruce, what in God's name are you doing?"

Bruce stopped. "I'm double-hauling, why?"

"That's not double-hauling. You look like you've got some kind of neuromuscular disorder. Come on, Bruce, we went over this last time we fished."

Crestfallen, Bruce lowered his fly rod. "I thought I was doing it right. What am I doing wrong?"

"Up, up, and out of the stream," said Lew. "See that grassy area over there? Get over there. I'll go through this again. Double-haul, my eye."

"But this is how you taught me last year."

"No, it is not. Now, watch me. We're going to go over this again."

Osborne, amused, leaned back against a large boulder to watch. Lew's black curls shone in the evening sun, her eyes soft shadows. When casting a fly rod, she moved with a grace that he never tired of watching.

"I want you to limit your power snap to a short arc, like this." Using Bruce's fly rod, Lew demonstrated what she meant. "Then on the back cast your line hand pulls the line in on the power snap . . . but gives it back while the line unrolls behind you."

She handed the fly rod back to Bruce and stood aside to watch him. "Good, that's a start. Now on the forward cast, your line hand should pull the line in on the power snap and give it back as the line rolls forward." Twice Bruce tried . . . and failed.

"You're getting there, but give me your rod." He handed it over. "Again," said Lew, "watch me."

Twice Lew executed the double-haul.

"I think I got it," said Bruce reaching for his fly rod to give the cast another try.

"Whoops, don't stiffen that hauling arm," said Lew. "Keep it flexed . . . okay, hold on. Try this, Bruce: think of the movement of your line hand being a recoil . . . Yes, better, much better.

"Okay, Bruce, you're getting there but stop thinking of all the mechanics and just let it happen. Trust your rod and line: Let yourself dance. That's what fly-casting is all about."

"Easy for you to say," said Bruce in a low grumble. He cast, trying hard, but his fly line collapsed in a heap.

"That's okay, Bruce. Don't give up. You will catch fish. I promise."

While Bruce struggled and Lew counseled, Osborne had stepped into the water and started to wade upstream where the evening sun was turning riffles into cascades of diamonds. With a roll cast he sent his trout fly into one of the scarlet pools beneath an overhang of tag alder. Once he lost sight and sound of Lew and Bruce, he could hear the rustle of trees preparing for the moon's arrival.

"Sorry, Chief, I need a rest."

The voice from downstream interrupted his reverie. Turning around, Osborne saw Bruce and Lew step up onto the stream bank, lay down their fly rods, and find places to sit among the boulders and swamp grass. Lew pulled a familiar-looking Ziploc from the front pocket of her waders: homemade gingersnaps.

"Save some for me," called Osborne as he waded in their direction.

"Well, what do you think, Chief?" asked Bruce. "That five-million-dollar life insurance policy makes it tough not to suspect the widow, doesn't it?" He was on his fourth cookie, which made Osborne happy he had arrived in time to grab three for himself.

Taking a bite of a gingersnap, Lew reflected on his comment. "Yeah, murder for hire is easier than you might think," she said.

"I'll never forget this man I knew years ago, a good friend of my grandfather's and someone who knew me when I was a kid. When he heard that my soon-to-be-ex-husband had belted me one, he offered to break both his legs. And he wasn't kidding. Took me awhile to calm him down."

"You might be right, Chief," said Bruce through his munching. "A buddy of mine who's a criminal defense lawyer in Wausau told me that when he did a stint in a DA's office while he was in law school, he couldn't get over the number of files on people who got caught trying to hire someone to do in their favorite person: their spouse in most cases.

"Problem is they hire someone who looks like they might want the business and that someone turns out to be undercover. He said you wouldn't believe how often that happens."

"Well, you two, I disagree with your theory on Karen Wright," said Osborne. "I've known Karen since she was a kid and I can tell you she is not that kind of person. She is a sweet, goodhearted individual. Always has been."

A fish jumped, relishing a caddisfly dessert. The three fishermen watched the rippling circles left behind.

"Whatever you say, Doc," said Bruce, "but personally I subscribe to the theory that people are not always who they appear to be."

"Based on forensic science?" teased Lew.

"Based on experience."

Chapter Eighteen

Mason looked up at the wall clock in her grandfather's kitchen. It was only seven P.M. and she didn't have to be at Ray's until eight thirty to help unload the fishing gear. Cool. Plenty of time to try out that kayak, maybe even meet Buster.

Being very careful, she lifted her grandfather's muskie rod and reel from the rack in his den. She wrapped the surface mudpuppy lure in paper towel so it wouldn't snag on anything and slipped it into her backpack.

The evening was so warm she hadn't bothered to change out of her shorts and T-shirt before running across the backyard, through the trees, and down the dirt lane to Ray's trailer. Just to be sure, she peered through the screen door into Ray's living room.

"Hey, Ray, it's me? Can I take the kayak out?" No answer. Oh well, he said he wouldn't mind.

She sat down at the picnic table to take off her sneakers and pull on her water shoes before hopping down to the dock where the little boat was tied along one side with bungee cords. After freeing the kayak, she held it with one hand while she waded into the water.

She slipped the muskie rod into the elastic holders that Ray had rigged to one side. Next she pushed her backpack down under the front of the boat where she would be able to reach it easily. She considered borrowing one of Ray's big fishing nets but she couldn't figure out how to attach the huge thing to the slender kayak; plus she figured if she got lucky—a big if, she knew—she could take a picture of her prize with her phone and then release it.

At the last minute, just as she was straddling the kayak and ready to plop down into the seat, Mason remembered the paddle. Oh my gosh that would have been a mistake. She giggled to herself as she grabbed the paddle off the dock.

Once in the boat and comfortable, she dipped the paddle into the stillness surrounding her. The afternoon breezes had died and the lake was placid, the only ripples coming from fish snacking on insects.

The kayak slipped through the water as silently as a mother duck. While she had fantasized calling out after Buster, she decided to wait on that. She pushed the kayak into the reeds until it became difficult to paddle. Mason set the paddle across the boat in front of her and reached down the side of the kayak to free the muskie rod. She attached the big yellow lure with all its hooks.

Just then a movement in the water off to the left of the front of the kayak caught her eye. Her heart stopped as the back of a creature as long as the kayak and spotted like a leopard surfaced less than two feet away only to disappear in an instant.

Had she seen that? Really? Or just imagined it? The water where the thing had disappeared held not even a ripple. She must have imagined it . . . no, she didn't. Maybe this was Buster? Ray had said the monster muskie guarded the weed bed.

Nah, had to be a big turtle. That's all. A big dumb turtle. She'd seen turtles that big at Brownie camp. Turtles are everywhere. But still . . .

Mason gritted her teeth and raised the heavy muskie rod up and back. The lure flew through the air, not very far, and landed with a loud plop. Better not let Ryan and Jake see that. They'll hoot. Gramps was right: she needed to practice. This wasn't easy.

She reeled in but when it was time to do the figure eight, she couldn't manage the move without getting up on her knees. The kayak wobbled beneath her. I wonder how deep it is here, thought Mason. Jeez, it would be easy to fall in.

She sat back down and raised the rod again. This time the lure flew higher, further. The rod bent with a tug so hard Mason had to grip the long rod handle with all her strength. She was holding on tight when she remembered Ray's instructions on reeling but as she started to do so, the tension in the fishing line eased.

Okay. Mason realized she'd been holding her breath and exhaled. Guess that's over. She was about to reel in more line when a creature that looked like a shark she had seen on TV flew into the air ten feet away, head shaking, water flying. Then it was gone and her line was running.

Oh boy. Would it charge the boat like Ray said?

Mason felt less terrified than determined not to do anything that could cause the fish to spit out the lure. She heard a rush of water and the rod tip danced as the fish surged, whipping its head in the air.

Two times she saw broad shoulders break the surface then disappear. She forgot to reel. All she could do was hold on. Do wolves swim? Do they live underwater? Maybe this wasn't a fish she had hooked after all. Maybe it was one of those weird creatures whose skeletons, picked clean by eagles, ended up on shore—smelly and frightening. The big boys in her neighborhood liked to tell scary stories about monsters living at the bottom of the lakes.

Refusing to panic, she remembered Ray's instruction to the boys if they were lucky enough to raise a big muskie: "If you don't put enough pressure on the line by pressing it with your index finger against the rod, you'll lose it but if you put too much pressure on, you might pop the leader or cause your rod sections to come apart. And remember, with a muskie, always expect the unexpected . . ."

Again the fish leapt into the air only to hit the water with a loud splash. Then the fish was gone, the line on the reel unspooling. She's at the bottom of the lake, thought Mason as she clung tight to the rod. This time the reel kept unspooling as the fish torpedoed its way through the reeds.

When all the line was out, Mason still held on.

Only then did she realize she was out of the reeds. The kayak was moving with the fish. Past a small bay and a scattering of cottages, the little boat slipped soundlessly across the water.

Staying deep now, the fish turned north, pulling Mason and the kayak up, up, up a channel that narrowed to a stream edged with cattails and tall grass. A rusted culvert loomed ahead. No way, thought Mason, no way me, the kayak, and the fish can make it through there together.

She had to decide: Ray's kayak or her grandfather's muskie rod?

If she lost the rod, it might be pulled along by the fish and never found. The kayak would land on shore somewhere. For sure someone would see it. Or she could get another job and buy Ray a new one. And she couldn't cut the line—she had no knife.

Pulling one strap of her backpack over her left shoulder and wobbling up onto her knees, Mason held the rod tight with both hands and tipped the kayak sideways until she could slip into the water. Rod out in front, she was drifting through the culvert when something felt wrong. Everything went slack. She had the rod but no fish.

On the far side of the long culvert, she struggled to find footing in the deep muck sucking at her feet. Struggling, she grabbed at tall grasses and pushed forward until she reached a muddy bank and could pull herself up. The area was dense with evergreens, their height eclipsing what sunlight remained.

Gosh, thought Mason. If it's this dark, it must be after nine. I'm really, really late. I need to call Ray. She reached into her backpack for her phone and clicked it on: *No Service.*

Osborne's cell phone rang just as he and Lew dropped Bruce off at the motel. Reaching for his phone in the top pocket of his shirt, Osborne slid sideways on the seat.

The three of them riding in the front seat in Lew's fishing truck had made him feel trapped between elbows. He needed air. Relieved, he answered the phone without checking to see who was calling.

"Doc, do you know where Mason is?" asked Ray in a worried voice.

"She's not with you?"

"No. She should have been here an hour ago. My fishing kayak is missing, too."

"I don't know what to say." Lew shot Osborne a questioning look.

"Now, don't worry, but you should know the boys and I just took a quick spin around the lake and no sign of her or the kayak."

"It's a big lake," said Osborne, knowing even as he spoke that the lake is not that big.

"I'll try her cell phone. Call you right back."

Mason's phone rang and rang and rang. Then her cheery voice: "Can't talk right now. Please leave a message."

Mason stumbled along the bank to where a grassy area ran over the culvert. She hoped to find a road there but there was no sign of one. Looking up, she could see telephone lines but the grass growing over the culvert sure looked like it hadn't been disturbed in ages. She was in the middle of nowhere.

Oh well, she thought, shouldering her backpack and holding the muskie rod with the handle out front and the rod pointed behind her in order to keep it from hitting branches, I better see if I can find a house or a road before it's pitch black out here.

Looking down at the creek that she'd climbed out of, she knew better than to get back into that. For one thing, she couldn't remember seeing any cabins or houses when she was being pulled along in the kayak. And there might be deep holes of muck in it, too.

Mason straightened her shoulders, looked up at the sky, and decided to walk what she figured had to be north. If west was the lake behind her and south was the other side of the creek, then north must lead back toward the road to cottages on Loon Lake. Into the woods she went.

She had been walking for a while when the forest gave way to what looked like a logging lane in the faint light of the rising moon. Okay, this has to go somewhere. At least the walking is easier. She could see ruts in the lane, which meant a four-wheeler or cart of some kind had been back here recently. She picked up her pace. If she was lucky she would find a house and they would have a regular phone.

Sure enough, she passed a log pile and just beyond it was a cabin. The windows were dark and there was no vehicle parked near it. Problem was it looked more like a hunting shack, one used only during deer season. Still, they might have a phone—her dad's hunting shack did.

Mason knocked on the door and waited. She wasn't surprised when there was no answer. She tried the doorknob. Locked. Mason set down her backpack and the fishing rod and walked around the small building. Peering through the windows she could see it was furnished and had a kitchen in one corner—oh, and a back door.

She ran around the building to the rear and moved two trashcans to one side of the door. She tried the knob. It turned but the door was stuck. She pushed hard and it opened. She peeked inside. A cardboard box had been shoved against the door. She pushed it away.

Safe! At least she wouldn't have to sleep in the woods. She reached for a wall switch and an overhead kitchen light went on. She hurried into the front room and searched for any sign of a phone but there was none. After unlocking the front door, she grabbed her backpack and the fishing rod to bring them safely inside.

The place was small but neat with an old sofa and a rocking chair facing a small fireplace. She collapsed onto the sofa and tried her cell phone again: *No Service.*

She was so tired from fighting the fish, she decided to close her eyes for a few minutes before heading outside again. She had to reach Ray and her grandfather.

Ray would probably fire her after this. Her grandpa would be so disappointed. Mason started to cry. Then she wiped her face with the sleeve of the sweatshirt she'd brought along in the backpack and tucked it behind her head as she laid on one arm of the sofa.

She woke what must be hours later. Though the moon was partially hid by trees, she could tell it had moved quite a distance from where it had been when she found the cabin. The night air was chill and she was shivering.

She found a chain on a little lamp beside the sofa and pulled. The light came on and she noticed for the first time that there was a small bathroom right off the kitchen. She used it and walking out saw there was another room right next to it.

Opening the door cautiously, Mason could see it was a bedroom. She flicked a light switch on the wall. The bed was a bare mattress though there was blanket and a set of sheets neatly folded at the foot. Needing something to keep her warm, she reached for the blanket and turning to switch off the light, she spotted a cluster of pictures pinned to the wall near the door.

Curious, she leaned forward to see what they were. That was a mistake. Without taking her eyes off one of the photos, she stood very still, listening. The pictures were so disturbing she wondered if the person who owned them was here, had been waiting for her to see these. She waited, every muscle tense.

But there was no sound. Mason backed out of the room and closed the bedroom door behind her. She went to the kitchen and got the cardboard box that had been in front of the back door. She shoved the box up against the bedroom door so the awfulness inside couldn't get out.

She tried to go back to sleep on the sofa. After a few minutes she knew that was hopeless. She shoved the sweatshirt into her backpack, stuck the phone in the back pocket of her shorts, grabbed the fishing rod and let herself out the front door of the cabin.

She made up her mind never to tell anyone what she had seen. If the person who owned the cabin knew she had seen those, they might do things to her, too.

She started down the dirt road only to stop. What if the owner of the cabin happens to drive back tonight? If she's walking here, they're sure to see her. Mason decided to stay off the dirt road but keep it in sight and hope that if someone did drive by, she would be hidden in the woods. The road was her only hope: it had to go somewhere.

Fortunately the trees in the forest were tall enough she could walk without wrecking Grandpa's muskie rod and right now only one thing mattered: She had to get out of here. Fast.

As she walked along, she remembered the pull of that huge fish. Wow, if she got out of here okay and not too many people were mad at her, wouldn't it be fun to go after Buster again? But no more fishing from a kayak for her. She'd learned that lesson. At least in a rowboat you can stand up without falling in.

And with that thought Mason realized she had lost sight of the dirt road.

Chapter Nineteen

Opening the back door and walking into the mudroom of Osborne's home, Lew heard an odd sound. She paused for a moment trying to figure out what it was she was hearing. Of course, and I'm not surprised, she thought. I would be crying, too.

Seated at the kitchen table with his head pressed face-down on his arms, which were crossed beneath him, Doc's shoulders were shaking, the strange sounds coming straight from his heart. Lew laid a hand softly on one shoulder as she spoke in a quiet tone. "Nothing new yet, Doc. I've got Todd and Roger out searching and the sheriff has pulled in six of his deputies."

Wiping at his face, Osborne shoved his chair back from the table. "I've got to call Erin." His voice cracked. "She needs to know this much. I can't call later when it's all over and I have to tell her the worst—"

"We don't know the worst, Doc. There may not be a 'worst.'" Lew pulled out the chair beside him and laid her arm across his shoulders as she sat down. "I think you should wait a while. Remember, Mason is a strong swimmer."

"Yes, but they found the kayak." He choked on his words. "No sign of her anywhere. Oh, God, why did I let her go? She's a little girl. So much she doesn't know."

"Yes, yes," said Lew, patting his shoulder, "but there's a lot she *does* know and that's why we're going to wait before you terrify her mother."

"Lewellyn, it is one o'clock in the morning and there is no sign whatsoever of an eleven-year-old child. What the hell can have happened?"

"Right." Lew was determined to calm his anguish. No matter what happened to Osborne's granddaughter she felt that alerting Erin and Mark in the middle of the night would be a serious mistake. The devastated parents would be sure to jump in their car and speed north, putting themselves at risk of a serious car accident.

"So here's what we're doing right now, Doc. First, the dive rescue team is scouring the entire area where Ray and the boys found the kayak. Meanwhile, my officers and the sheriff's deputies have made a grid ten miles square and they are driving every passable road because we think she's lost in the woods somewhere. They have the K-nine search dogs with them, too."

"I don't know why the hell you think she's in the woods somewhere," Osborne challenged. "We know she fell out of the goddamn boat, for Chrissake."

"Okay, you keep thinking that. But I disagree and I'll tell you why—"

Lew's cell phone rang just then. "Yes, Dani, any news from the nine-one-one dispatch centers? Oh, okay. Yes, keep trying. Stay in touch with all six centers. I know some are a ways away but on the chance that a cell tower might route the call . . . Good, thank you."

"No calls, right?" asked Osborne.

"Correct, but I expected that. Doc, two things are likely. Either she dropped her cell phone in the water so it's ruined and she can't call. Or wherever she is, there is no cell service—and she can't call.

You know yourself that once you're a couple miles out of town, cell service is spotty to say the least.

"And even if Mason does call nine-one-one it's likely she won't be able to tell them where she is because she herself won't know. The poor kid is lost. And the nine-one-one dispatchers have no way to pinpoint the exact location where a call is coming from. All they know is the cell tower through which the call was routed. Doc, I'm sorry but technology is great until it isn't."

"I wish you hadn't told me that," said Osborne, his eyes dark.

"Going back to what I was saying before Dani called, the reason I think she has to be lost somewhere on land is because that kid is spunky. I've watched her. She's an excellent swimmer, she's strong, she's a runner, and she grew up in Loon Lake. She's been in the outdoors forever.

"*Mason is going to find her way.* I mean, if I were her I would and I got lost a couple times when I was a kid."

Osborne mustered a slight smile. "I did, too, now that I think about it." He took a deep breath. "You are giving me hope."

"And you did hear that Ray demanded that the fishing tournament be suspended until she's found. He's rounded up all the participating boats and has them out searching every bay and tributary connecting to Loon Lake. The sheriff's department outfitted all those boats with floodlights, too. If Mason is anywhere near water, trust me, they'll find her."

Osborne nodded and his shoulders seemed to relax ever so slightly.

"Mind if I say something off the subject for a moment, Doc?"

"Go right ahead, though I doubt it'll do any good."

"I got a call on my cell about four hours ago. Nina Krezminski."

"Oh, jeez. What the hell did she want?"

"Nina seems to think she's solved our double homicide . . ."

"You must be kidding."

"Oh no," said Lew, trying for a lighter tone in her voice, "she alleges she heard Fred Smith tell Joyce that Chet told him he was planning to fire Joyce.

"Nina forgot about that until this evening. I called Joyce to ask her if she had spoken with Nina recently and Joyce said that because the club is still under restrictions as a crime scene, she refused to let Nina enter to take any personal belongings.

"This is the second time she has tried that and, according to Joyce, Nina got pretty upset. So I'll put Nina's comments in my reports, but I have to say I am prejudiced. The way I see it, Joyce Harmon has everything to lose with what happened. I'm sure the closing of Buddy's Place reduces her pay, for starters. That poor woman is desperate to keep her job and she needs every penny she makes. Good try, Nina."

Lew could see Osborne wasn't listening.

"You know, Lew," he said with a distant look in his eye, "after we got that call from Ray and while you were working with the sheriff's department, I walked down to the dock just after the sun had set tonight. There was a glorious haze of violet and gold and all I could think was that a God who makes a sky like that does not let children die." He wept.

Lew ducked her head so he wouldn't see the worry in her eyes. After several minutes, she managed to say, "Come on, Doc, why don't you move to the living room and lie down on the couch? See if you can close your eyes. You look exhausted. I'll stay awake in case we get a call."

"Lewellyn, you have just asked me to do the impossible. I am not moving from this room."

"Then I'll make us both a fresh pot of coffee." Lew got up from the kitchen table.

"That sounds good," said Osborne, the tears flowing down his cheeks. She reached over to pull him into her arms.

His silent shuddering reminded her of that night five years ago when she was called to identify the body of her dead son. Dear God, she prayed, please don't let that happen again.

Chapter Twenty

Like he did every morning except Sunday, Herm Jensen leapt out of bed at five A.M. He wanted to be headed to town by five thirty. In the two years since his wife died, he had come to relish these mornings: early coffee at McDonald's with men he had known for years. It was the best way ever to start his day.

Only those guys could make him laugh so hard he worried he might die in the midst of a guffaw. But what a way to go that would be. Half his buddies were widowers like himself; the other half insisted they had wives they dreaded facing so early in the morning. At least that's what they alleged. Good guys, every one.

Herm whistled as he finished dressing, fed his golden, and hopped into the front seat of his late wife's Highlander. Still whistling, he sped down the driveway from the little ranch home that he and Mildred had built for their retirement years.

Like he did every morning as he drove past the hedge of blooming mock orange bushes that Mildred had loved, he questioned the wisdom of living alone so far out in the country. But he loved driving past the open potato fields that surrounded his house and the spring-fed streams carrying tannins from wetlands crammed with tamarack and tag alder that meandered along the narrow roadway before spilling into big old Loon Lake.

As he turned right onto the county road, he saw a young girl in shorts and a T-shirt, a backpack slung over one shoulder, walking along the shoulder with her back to him. She was carrying a good-sized fishing rod. That's odd. To the best of his knowledge there are no fish in the creek near the road.

Maybe she's waiting for the school bus? But it's summer and the kids are out of school. Hmm. He made sure to take a good look as he passed her.

Whoa, wait a minute. Herm threw his car into reverse, backed up, and lowered the passenger side window. "Miss Mason," he called out, "what the goldarnheck are you doing out here this time of day?"

An expression of relief mixed with happiness flooded across the girl's face. She ran up to the car. "Uncle Herm? Ohmygosh, I'm so lost. Would you mind? I mean, can you give me a ride back to Grandpa's, please?"

"What do you mean you're lost?" he asked as she opened the rear door to lay her fishing rod at a careful angle across the dog bed in the back seat. "Hey, isn't that your grandpa's muskie rod with that precious Garcia Ambassadeur Reel of his? I keep trying to buy that dang thing off of him. What the heck are you doing with that, young lady?"

Concern struck him and he asked, "Is your grandfather okay? Has something happened? What on earth?"

"Gramps is fine. Just me. I'm the one in trouble," said Mason.

Climbing into the front seat beside the old man, she started to tell her story.

Mason knew Herman Jensen well. He was one of the two widowed men whom her grandfather had brought to their house on cold Saturday nights for her mom's chili dinners a couple of times. He was very nice. And he liked to tease, calling her "Miss Mason." She usually made a face when he did that but not this morning.

After stumbling through the woods, wading through two rock-strewn brooks, and managing to cross a potato field without spraining an ankle, she was happy to be called anything.

"Yeah, so I was fishing on Loon Lake not far from Grandpa's house when I hooked this big muskie and it pulled the kayak way, away from the lake—"

"Stop, honey," said Herm, patting her knee. "When did this happen exactly?"

"Last night. About seven fifteen, I think."

"You've not been home since?"

"No but I'm staying at Grandpa's while Mom and Dad and Cody are in Madison."

"So your grandfather doesn't know where you are?"

As he asked the question he vaguely remembered waking to the sound of sirens during the night. Searchers he would bet. Doc Osborne must be frantic.

"Huh-uh. I've been trying to call him on my cell phone but it keeps saying *No Service*." As she spoke, Mason reached into the backpack at her feet and pulled out a cell phone. "I'll try now though . . . nope, still won't work. It's charged. I can see it's charged. Wouldn't you think it would work if it's charged, Uncle Herm?"

"Golly," said Herm, "I wish you had found my house. I have a landline." For one second he thought about turning around but decided against that. "Okay, we need to get in touch with your grandfather ASAP. So two more miles down the road here and we'll have cell service at that new Kwik Trip they just built by Highway Seventeen. We'll stop there and call. Save your story for when we get you to your grandpa, kid."

"Yeah and I need to be at work pretty soon, too."

"We'll worry about that later." Herm could not resist a silent chuckle. What was this girl thinking?

He swung into the gas station parking area. Mason had her cell phone out and was delighted to hear her call going through.

"Grandpa?"

"Mason?" Osborne jumped to his feet, waving at Lew who had fallen asleep in the armchair across from him. "Where? What?"

"I'm okay. I got lost but Uncle Herm picked me up—"

Herm took the phone from Mason. "Doc, she's fine. We're on our way to your place. Be there in about ten minutes. Looks like she spent the night in the woods out by my place. Guess we better make her an Eagle Scout, huh?"

Mike greeted them with joyful barking as Herm pulled into Osborne's driveway and parked next to the Loon Lake Police cruiser. Osborne opened the back door and ran toward Mason.

"Mason, are you okay? I've been worried sick and Chief Ferris, the sheriff's department—everyone's been searching for you."

"I know, I was so afraid, Grandpa." Mason wrapped her arms around Osborne's chest and burst into tears. "But I found Uncle Herm so I'm okay now."

"Oh, thank God you're all right." He held her away from him, looking her up and down as if to be sure she hadn't lost an arm or a leg. "I'll bet you're hungry, huh? Lew's got bacon and eggs going. Raisin toast, too. Herm, come on in. We are celebrating."

"Hey, you. For the record? You are not allowed to do that ever again, you hear? I'm the Loon Lake chief of police and I demand—" Before Lew could finish, Mason gave her a huge hug and a grin. "Watch the apron," said Lew, pretending to gasp for air.

With a quick call to her dispatcher, she had been able to get out the news that Mason was safe. "You have no idea, Mason, how many people have been up all night searching for you. Your grandpa hasn't slept. I haven't slept. I don't think Ray and the entire tournament crowd has gotten any sleep."

"I need to call Ray right now," said Mason jumping up from her chair. "He needs me to work this morning."

"You go ahead and call. But you might have to wake him up," said Osborne, hiding a smile. He had been able to reach Ray and Erin right after hearing Mason's voice. Erin, who had known nothing until he woke her up, was insisting on renting a car and driving north as soon as possible that morning.

"Ray?" Mason had him on the phone. "I'm sorry I'm late but I'll be right over . . ." She listened, then said, "Oh, okay. I'll be over then and sorry about last night. Did you catch any fish, 'cause I got a big one but she got away. Sure, tell you all about it later."

She sat back down at the kitchen table, happy. "I don't work until tonight," she said.

"I thought that might be the case," said her grandfather. "Now tell us about this big fish and just exactly what happened."

When she had finished describing the fish—how it rolled and shook, how it charged at her then ran deep, how it bit through the fishing line and left her stranded in the creek—Osborne, Lew, and Herm sat silent.

"Tell us again what that muskie looked like," said Osborne.

"I saw this fat back and it was as long as the paddle I was using."

"You hooked Buster," said Osborne. "You hooked our superfish, girl. To pull you along in that kayak like she did, she had to weigh forty-five, maybe fifty pounds."

"No, Grandpa, Buster hooked me. She ate your lure, too. After Ray pays me, I have to buy you a new one."

"We'll see about that," said Osborne. "Right now you eat hearty and then I want you to take a nice long nap."

"Speaking of which," said Lew, "I need the same, so if you will excuse me, I'm going to head over to my place and get some rest.

But, first, I have a couple questions, Mason. That kayak you were in. Sounds like it was not real stable. I'm going to check with Ray and try it out myself. We don't need another extreme fishing experience like the one you just had."

"It paddles great," said Mason. "Only problem was when I got up on my knees to try to reel in. That's when it got real shaky. I had to sit down or fall out."

"Hmm. Maybe kayaks like that aren't made for fishing muskies. My other question is about that cabin you found. Was it unlocked? I need to know if you had to break the lock in case someone reports a break-in."

A flash of fear riveted Mason. Whatever she was asked, she wouldn't tell about the awful pictures in that room.

"It's okay. You won't be held responsible but I need to find that cabin and let the owners know why you had to use it. That's all. But we can talk about that later."

"I'm not sure I can find it," said Mason. "I had to walk a long ways after I left." She paused before deciding to lie. "I did a good job locking it up when I left. I really didn't touch anything except get a drink of water and use the bathroom. They won't even know I was there, Chief Ferris."

"Don't worry about that now. Get some rest."

Chapter Twenty-One

Erin arrived at Osborne's before noon and raced down the stairs to her old bedroom. She cracked the door: Mason was sound asleep. Reassured, she crept back up the stairs and hurried into the kitchen.

"Mason's okay, right?" asked Osborne, who was waiting for her at the kitchen table.

"She's fine. Sound asleep but, Dad, you look terrible."

Coming up from behind her father, Erin bent over to give him a fierce hug. Eyes closed tight with emotion, Osborne rested both hands on hers. "Thank you, Erin. You cannot imagine how worried I've been."

"Brought back memories of that night Mom died, I'll bet," she said of the evening Mary Lee's bronchitis had turned deadly and Osborne, with the help of Ray Pradt (in spite of Mary Lee's longstanding animosity toward him), rushed her to the hospital in the midst of a howling blizzard.

"No, Erin, this was worse, much worse."

Still stricken by the thought of possibly losing his granddaughter, Osborne couldn't say more. What he was thinking, though, was the loss of Mary Lee, who had lived her life exactly as she wanted it, did not compare to losing a child as precious as Mason, a young girl with all life's wonders ahead of her. Nope, no comparison.

"You need to know, Dad, this could just as easily have happened to me and Mark. You told me yourself once: the minute you give birth to a child you take the risk of something awful happening."

"But if I hadn't been out fly-fishing . . ."

"Dad," said Erin in a warning tone, "do not go there. Mason was determined to go after that fish whether you were home or not. I know my child and once she makes her mind up . . . stay out of her way."

Osborne managed a slight grin. "You're making me feel better, kiddo."

"Good." Erin unwrapped her arms from around him and pulled out one of the kitchen chairs to sit down.

"Oh and, Dad, Mark asked me if there are any significant developments on those homicides out at Buddy's Place? He won't be back in the office until tomorrow and he's been hoping not to call in during Cody's soccer tournament. You know how that goes—one phone call and he's back as the DA instead of soccer dad."

"Significant? Not that I am aware. As of late yesterday, Bruce had no results back from his techs at the crime lab yet. The crime lab pathologists have the two autopsies underway. Meanwhile, among other pieces of evidence, Bruce is waiting on a footprint analysis, which may prove critical to identifying a suspect. Also, Ray found a wireless deer cam with a hazy image that Bruce is hoping the crime lab's digital equipment can sharpen.

"I am sure Lew will know more later today, but we were both up all night so she was hoping to catch some sleep this morning. But one interesting fact did surface during an interrogation of the three members of the Deer Creek Preserve who say they were victims of credit card fraud out at the club.

"One of the three, a man named Bert Bronk, alleges Karen Wright is the beneficiary of a five-million-dollar life insurance policy in the event of Chet's death. Lew has asked me to help her check that out later today."

Erin stared at her father. "That's a lot of money."

"Maybe too much?"

"Oh, c'mon, Dad, I cannot imagine Karen being involved in anything remotely like what that question implies. Keep in mind she is only two years older than me and we've known each other since grade school.

"And, Dad, Karen's a good egg, always has been."

"Do you run into her often?" asked Osborne.

"Yes, I mean I used to. Up until recently she had been golfing with a bunch of us on Ladies Day at the country club but now that I think of it, she hasn't been there at all this spring.

"The few times I've run into her lately, she has seemed pretty . . . subdued." Erin paused for a moment, then said, "That's a good way to put it: subdued. But, Dad, really. If I had to describe Karen Wright in one word? Genuine. She is a genuine, good person."

If only that counted, thought Osborne.

"And I'm not saying good people don't do bad things but Karen has always come across as goodhearted. And brave. Remember how she might have been killed herself when she saved that little boy's life?"

"When was that, Erin? About twenty-five years ago? I remember it was over a school holiday of some kind."

"Washington's Birthday. You and Mom were away at a dental convention and we had a babysitter, which is why I remember it so well. That's because our babysitter was old Mrs. Schultz and I remember thinking at the time there was no way she could have rescued us like Karen did the Smith kid."

"Was it a house fire?"

"An explosion *and* a fire. Karen's family lived right next door to the Smiths. They had a ton of kids and Fred was the youngest.

I think he was maybe four years old. He was home all by himself in an upstairs bedroom when a gas leak somewhere in the house caused an explosion that blew out the kitchen windows before the kitchen caught fire.

"Karen was outside and saw it happen. She ran into the house, up the stairs, and grabbed the little kid but when she turned to go down the entire stairwell was in flames. She was able to climb out an upstairs window and sat on the roof or something with little Fred.

"People who were watching said later that the firemen rescued them just in time, like a few seconds before the whole house caught fire."

"Boy, I'd forgotten about that," said Osborne. "So that was the Smith family was it?"

"Yeah. The little boy? That's Fred Smith. He's still around somewhere. Quite the odd bird, too. I heard from my friend Denise, who used to teach at the middle school, that back in the day he tested off the charts for the gifted program but he was socially inept—a total misfit. Karen has always impressed me that she's been so kind to the guy all these years."

Erin checked her watch. "Dad, I hate to wake Mason right now. She's out cold."

"Please don't. She'll be heartbroken if she can't finish her job helping Ray. She's due to help tonight at eight when he and the two boys get back from their day of fishing. Then the tournament winds up tomorrow morning at ten. I think she should stay one more night here with me."

"But if you have to meet with Chief Ferris soon why don't I wait here until she wakes up, run her home for dinner, and have her back in time for Ray and the boys. Sound good?"

"That works. Thanks for the background on Karen—I'd forgotten all that."

At three that afternoon, and feeling better than earlier that day, Osborne sat down with Bruce and Lew in her office. Bruce led off the meeting.

"I have bad news and good news. The best the guys can do with the video from the deer cam is that you're seeing a partial view of an individual who appears to be five feet seven inches tall. Not enough for an estimate on weight or if the image is male or female. Sorry.

"As far as the clothing goes, not much help either except that it was dark. Not camouflage either, just dark clothing. The other disappointing news is that we can't get more prints off the lever that hoisted the piano. Not yet anyway. There is some new technology over in Europe that might help but it's going to take time for those results."

"But you do have good news?" asked Lew hopefully.

"Yes, the footprints have come through loud and clear. They confirmed what I predicted: You are looking for someone who was wearing a pair of Vasque hiking boots, men's size ten."

Bruce sat back with a happy grin. "Pretty good on that, huh?"

"At least it isn't a Nike sneaker," said Lew. "Everyone in Loon Lake owns a pair of those."

"Otherwise, Chief, Rich and I are finishing up at Buddy's Place. Ray Pradt did another pass outdoors and said he didn't find anything other than signs indicating there had been a four-wheeler or golf cart pulled up behind the club in recent days. Could be the individual seen on the deer cam video. Ray did say he got good photos of tracks around the building, too.

"As far as evidence gathering, we've done it. We'll catch a bite to eat at the Loon Lake Pub and head home. Sound good?"

"Thanks, Bruce," said Lew. "You just gave me a good reason to make a surprise visit to the grieving widow."

"The one I hear is going to be worth five million?"

"Now, where did you hear that?" asked Lew, exasperated. "I haven't said a word to anyone."

"That one fellow who's a member of the Deer Creek Preserve, the big one, Bert. He sat at a table by Rich and me this morning while we were having breakfast at the motel. He's got a voice so loud no one in the breakfast room could miss hearing every word.

"Fellow was pretty vocal on the life insurance. You think *that* news hasn't gotten around town?"

Lew looked over at Osborne. "If you aren't too tired, old man, I think we need to stop by Karen's house and let her know that as the sole proprietor of Buddy's Place now, she needs to be sure it's locked up—and she needs my approval before she can do that."

Chapter Twenty-Two

During the drive out to the Wright home Osborne asked, "Lewellyn, what is the real reason for our surprise visit this afternoon? You could have made a phone call to let Karen know the club was ready to be locked up."

"True, but the real reason is I'm debating when to tell her we're convinced that her husband and Tiffany were murdered. Until I do that, I'd like her to assume we're still considering the possibility that her husband was killed in a tragic, unexpected accident."

"But why not tell her what is obvious to us and to the Wausau boys? She'll find out soon enough if she doesn't know already."

"I could be wrong, but my thinking is that if I don't make her feel like she's a prime suspect, she's likely to be more open, even helpful."

"Ah," said Osborne, "good point. I would add that there is something to be said about observing a person in her own environment. You can learn a lot about someone when you see how they live, what's important to them."

"Like you enjoying hours on your dock in the moonlight—"

"Or you carving little wooden eagles and owls for your grandchildren.

"We are two very different people, aren't we, Chief Ferris?" teased Osborne. He turned away to gaze out the car window as he said with a mock sigh, "I guess that's why we'll never marry."

"Now who said that," Lew answered with a grin. "Don't you know it's the suspense that keeps us together?

"Oops, we are almost there, Doc. Just so you know I do not want to bring up the life insurance right away. See if she brings it up instead."

"Good point. Meantime, after what I saw yesterday, I'd like to know more about her relationship with Dr. Pete Kretzler," said Osborne. "I find that curious."

Lew pulled into the circle driveway and parked alongside a dark green Range Rover. Osborne followed her up the granite steps that led to the front door of Karen Wright's home. The door swung open before they could even knock.

Karen stood in the doorway, surprise on her face. "Oh, gosh, you startled me. I just walked in and heard someone coming up the stairs. Did you call to say you were coming? My phone has been off all afternoon. I was in the middle of a photo shoot for the class I'm teaching. So I'm sorry if—"

"No messages," said Lew. "Dr. Osborne and I need to talk with you about several new developments in our investigation and that is always easier in person. I was hoping we could catch you at home."

"Well, you have," said Karen, opening the door wider and motioning for them to enter. "Chief Ferris, Dr. Osborne, please come in but excuse me while I get out of these boots of mine. I don't want to track swamp mud everywhere."

She walked over to an oak bench against one wall in the large foyer and sat down to pull off what appeared to be hiking boots clogged with dried mud along with two pairs of crew socks before slipping on a pair of moccasins. Even though the day was quite warm, she was in jeans and a black sweatshirt.

"Sorry if I look a mess but I dress to avoid mosquitoes and black flies. The heron rookery may be lovely to look at but it is treacherous to walk through: you can get eaten alive or drown in a pothole of muck. Have either of you been there? It is a beautiful spot."

"I don't know that I've heard of it," said Osborne.

"Me neither," said Lew. "Where is it exactly?"

"Ah, it's one of the best kept secrets of Deer Creek," said Karen. "Fred showed it to me earlier this spring. He thought it would be a good subject for my outdoor photography class and he was right. I have been able to shoot a family of great blue herons from when the eggs were laid to the chicks hatching. Can you believe it?"

Karen gave them a soft smile as she beckoned them down a hallway to her kitchen. "Coffee? Tea, or a soft drink?"

"Not for me, I'm fine," said Lew.

"Me neither but thank you," said Osborne as he climbed onto one of the tall stools surrounding a butcher-block island in the center of the kitchen. "Did you say it was Fred Smith who showed you the heron rookery?"

"Yes. Right after he took over running maintenance for Deer Creek, he stumbled onto the rookery when he was searching for mushrooms. Fred *loves* wild mushrooms," said Karen with another smile. "Me? I'm terrified of 'em.

"But that's how he found the rookery and since then he and Ty Wallis have managed to restrict any hunting around that area, thank goodness."

While she was talking, Karen had poured herself a large glass of water and now sat down across from Lew and Osborne, elbows on the butcher-block surface as she rested her chin in one hand, features relaxed. Osborne could see she had gotten some good sun that day.

"You said you're here with news about the accident?" she asked Lew.

"Yes and to let you know that your husband's remains will be released to the funeral home sometime tomorrow. But Dr. Osborne and I have questions for you on other aspects of the tragedy.

"I hope this isn't a bad time to talk, Karen. We realize you've had quite a shock, a lot to deal with. Also, because there hasn't been a legal ruling on whether your husband's death is the result of an accident or foul play, I will be tape-recording our conversation. Dr. Osborne and I may also take notes. I hope that doesn't bother you too much."

While she was talking, Lew set the tape recorder on the counter between them and pulled her notebook from her back pocket.

"Heavens, no. Whatever you need to do is fine. I understand this is official so, please, go right ahead. But you're right, the last forty-eight hours have been . . . difficult."

Karen raised her eyebrows as she gazed down at the butcher-block pattern in front of her. "I'll tell you what makes it hard is not having any close family members around like most people do when there's an unexpected death.

"Chet's folks are gone, my folks are gone, I was an only child and then Chet and I never had children. Of course," she said, sounding a little brighter, "I do have Fred to help out. He's like a brother, a little brother."

"You saved his life years ago, didn't you," said Osborne sympathetically.

"Yes and we've been close ever since, although he used to drive Chet bonkers always being so precise and, well, 'tight-assed,' as Chet would say, about everything. That's why he's working at Deer Creek now.

"I had hired him to be our handyman here but Fred was just too much for Chet. While poor Fred thought he was keeping everything in perfect working order, Chet thought he was being a busybody. The final straw was Fred 'tidying up' Chet's precious 1927 Chris-

Craft powerboat when he'd been told not to go near it. I'd told him to leave it alone, too, but Freddie can be selective in what he hears.

"Been that way since he was a kid. Fred is definitely quirky," said Karen, "but he is so creative. Suggesting I shoot the rookery was brilliant—no one applying for an MFA has a portfolio like mine."

She got up to refill her glass. "Working at Deer Creek put just the right amount of distance between one of the people dear to me and my husband."

"Sounds like Fred adores you," said Lew.

"He knows how to make me feel good when I have a down day," said Karen with an appreciative laugh.

She pushed the glass of water away as she spoke. "Be nice if he could find himself a girlfriend one of these days. He deserves more family than just me—which I keep telling him. But Fred has always been a loner." Karen shrugged. "Probably always will be. Some people are just like that, y'know."

A serious look crossed her face. "He didn't have much of a family life growing up and that can make a difference. Maybe you remember this, Dr. Osborne, but Fred was the youngest of eleven kids. They lived next door to us and, boy, that place was a mess. Junk in the yard, dogs always on the loose.

"My mom couldn't stand how their garbage was always overflowing onto our driveway. She called the health department on them a couple times. The parents were never home. Fred's dad worked at the mill and his mom waited tables somewhere so he was always by himself or trying to tag along after the big kids. Then there was the rumor that the mom got pregnant by another man and Fred was the result. Who knows if that was true?

"Boy, I'll never forget the day their house blew up. It was in the afternoon and I was getting my bike out of our garage when I saw all the windows at the back of the house blow out. I could hear screaming and I knew that had to be little Freddie.

"I didn't even think—I just ran. In the front door, up this big circular stairway that was right there and found Freddie in an upstairs bedroom. Terrified. I pushed him out the window in front of me 'cause there was kind of a shaky old sleeping porch with no screens and that's where we were when the fire engines came. We were both lucky."

"You were pretty darn brave for a twelve-year-old girl," said Osborne. "Erin remembers that day."

"There are times you don't think, you just do what you have to do. If it had been Erin there, I'll bet you she would have done the same," said Karen. "She's a good golfer, by the way."

"Sorry to change the subject," said Lew, interrupting, "but getting back to what we have been hoping was an accident at Buddy's Place, I need to alert you that the forensic team from the Wausau Crime Lab finished up their work at Buddy's Place late this afternoon. People can now enter but I am sure you will want to have someone lock up the property."

"That will be Fred. As soon as possible, I'm going put it on the market," said Karen, her tone grim. "I don't want to see that place, go near it ever again. Though I can't imagine anyone will want to buy it now. Maybe I should have it torn down and sell the land."

"Karen," said Lew, "I think it is critical you be aware that the forensic experts from the Wausau Crime Lab who been have gathering evidence at the club do not believe your husband and Tiffany Niedermeier died as the result of an accident.

"Now that all the evidence at the scene has been collected, documented, and secured, Bruce Peters from the Wausau Crime Lab is convinced your husband and his friend were murdered."

"Do you think that?" Karen's eyes widened and her body tensed. "That someone murdered my husband and that stripper? Is that really what *you* think? Dr. Osborne?"

"I'm not sure what to think just yet," said Lew. "If that is the case then the question for law enforcement is this: Was your husband the target and did the woman with him just happen to be in the wrong place at the wrong time? Or did someone want both of them dead?"

"Well," Karen waved a dismissive hand, "I don't see how anyone can begin to think that? I mean, how could a person even dream up such a way of killing someone? Chief Ferris, I hate to disagree with your supposed experts but in my opinion they are wrong."

Aware this might be a good time to try to keep the conversation on a more positive note, Osborne asked, "I have a question, Karen. What do you remember of Monday night?"

"You mean before you found Chet and . . ."

"Yes. What were you doing and where?" asked Osborne.

"Gosh," said Karen, "nothing special really. I was here working on lesson plans. I've told you that Chet and I have been living separate lives so he's been sleeping in the guesthouse. When he's been here, that is. I stopped trying to keep track of his coming and going months ago." Again, the soft, disarming smile.

"I went to bed early. I like to read and be asleep by ten at the latest."

"Did anyone stop by or call you that evening?" asked Lew. "Your friend, Fred, perhaps?"

"No, I was all by myself that night. Then Tuesday morning I saw my divorce lawyer and I was driving back here when Ty called with the awful news. That's when I drove out to the club and met up with you and Dr. Osborne—"

Before Karen could say more, her cell phone rang. She looked at the number. "It's my therapist. Do you mind if I take the call? Just need to make an appointment."

"Go right ahead," said Lew. "May I use your powder room?"

"Of course. It's across from the foyer by the front door."

Lew left the kitchen while Karen walked over to the nearby counter, phone in hand, and jotted something onto a notepad there. Lew was back by the time she was off the phone.

"Do I take it you know Dr. Kretzler, the hand surgeon from Milwaukee? Good friend of Chet's . . . and yours?" asked Osborne.

"Y-e-e-s-s," said Karen, "why?"

"When we met with Dr. Kretzler and the other two Deer Creek members who say there are credit card issues connected to Buddy's Place, Dr. Kretzler was very concerned for you. He was quite taken aback with something Bert Bronk shared about Chet's gambling."

Osborne paused. He didn't want to bring up the life insurance until Lew was ready to do so herself.

"Pete and I dated one summer," said Karen. "He was working as a camp counselor outside of Eagle River and we met at the Cellar Bar. You know, the big hangout for camp counselors in the day. It was my freshman year in college and Chet was in Europe with his folks. We only dated a short time—then Chet was back.

"So, yes, I've known Pete and his wife over the years, since we're all members of the Deer Creek Preserve. I'm sure Pete knows I had nothing to do with Chet's shenanigans. What did Bert Bronk have to say that bothered Pete?"

Osborne caught Lew's eye: she would take it from here.

"Mr. Bronk said that you took out a five-million-dollar life insurance policy on your husband. He said you wouldn't allow him to play baccarat in Las Vegas without it. Is that true? Will you be paid that kind of money now that Chet is dead?"

"Yes, I will," said Karen without blinking an eye.

"But Bert Bronk has it all wrong. I didn't take out the policy. The casino in Las Vegas insisted that Chet take out life insurance on both of us. Five million on him, five million on me, and for good reason. Chet wanted to sit at the baccarat table where the bets are often in the million-dollar range or more.

"The casino knows how fast money can be lost and they want to be sure that if there is an accident or a heart attack or an angry estranged spouse that they will be paid what they are owed. Does that make sense?"

"Yes," said Lew.

"I am well aware that I appear to be the angry estranged spouse—but do I also look stupid?"

The kitchen was quiet.

"Here's something to share with Mr. Bronk, Chief Ferris, because I know right where he's going with this," said Karen, her tone hardening as she spoke.

"Chet Wright owes so much money and as his still-legal spouse I now owe that money so that when all his debts are settled I doubt, seriously doubt, there will be much left of the five million. I will still be selling this house. I will still be working."

"I appreciate your candor, Karen," said Lew as she slid off the stool and onto her feet. "But I do have to inform you that you are considered 'a person of interest' in the death of your husband and Tiffany Niedermeier."

"And what does that mean exactly? Am I under arrest?" Karen looked flabbergasted.

"No. But it does mean that you cannot leave Loon Lake until our investigation is complete. I'm sorry to say that includes no teaching in Rhinelander as well." Lew picked up the tape recorder and slipped her notebook back into her pocket.

"I see. Chief Ferris, Dr. Osborne," said Karen, standing up to extend a hand to Lew and to Osborne, "I am confident you will find me innocent."

Lew shook her hand. "Karen, thank you for your time this afternoon."

Back in the cruiser, Lew pulled out of the driveway and drove 500 feet before pulling onto the shoulder far enough to be out of sight from the Wright's front door. She reached for her cell phone.

"Dispatch? Is Dani still in? Please put her on . . . Dani, I need you to pull up the boilerplate for a search warrant, print three copies, and set them on my desk, please. I'll be there in ten minutes and fill in the specifics.

"But first, please call the judge's chambers in the courthouse and ask the secretary to let the judge know I'll be by shortly with a search warrant for him to sign. Ask her to be sure he doesn't leave until I get there. This cannot wait for tomorrow. Thank you."

She hit another number on her phone.

"Bruce, you're still in town, right? Good. I'll meet you at the Loon Lake Pub in an hour and don't you dare leave before I get there. I have new evidence for you to take with you tonight . . . Sorry, tell you when I get there. I'm rushing to get a search warrant right now." She clicked off and put the cruiser in gear.

"You haven't fooled me," said Osborne. "You didn't use the powder room, did you?"

Lips pressed tight, Lew gave him the dim eye. "When was the last time you saw me take a bathroom break in the middle of an interrogation?"

"Those boots she was wearing—Vasque?"

"Yep."

"Very interesting. I'm surprised though."

"You said it yourself, Doc. Good people . . ."

"I know, I know. Still I am surprised. And I hope you don't mind but I need to head home, Lew. I promised Erin I would be there for Mason's last night working with Ray and the boys."

Chapter Twenty-Three

Lew raced into her office. It was almost four thirty and she knew Judge Dickson liked to leave his office by then. The three copies of the search warrant were on her desk with Dani waiting to see if she needed anything more. Lew looked down. "No, this is fine, and thank you."

"The judge promised to wait for you," said Dani.

"Great," said Lew as she started to write in the specifics. That took less than five minutes and she was back out the door and around the building to the courthouse.

Pulling into Karen's driveway twenty minutes later, Lew was relieved to see the Ranger Rover was still there. She hurried up the stairs to the front door and rang the doorbell. She wanted to get this over as soon and as easily as possible.

Karen was at the door within seconds. "Chief Ferris, did you forget something?"

"No, I have a search warrant, Karen."

"*A search warrant?* You mean to search my house?" she asked.

"Not your house. I have a search warrant that allows me to confiscate one item of evidence from your front foyer. Please let me by," said Lew.

"Well . . . okay," said Karen, stepping back with a baffled look on her face. She watched as Lew pulled on a pair of nitrile gloves, picked up the hiking boots, which were right where Karen had left them earlier, and slipped the boots into an evidence bag.

"Thank you, Karen, I appreciate your cooperation."

Karen, bewildered, said nothing as Lew ran back down the steps to the police cruiser.

Bruce was just tucking into his meatloaf and mashed potatoes when Lew rushed into the Loon Lake Pub main dining room. Since five fifteen is early for most diners, the room was empty except for Bruce and Rich. Lew set a cardboard box holding the evidence bag on the floor beside his chair.

"What's that?" asked Bruce, his fork in midair.

"Confiscated these at the Wright residence. They were worn this afternoon by Mrs. Wright."

"And?"

"Vasque hiking boots, men's size ten."

"But you just said Karen Wright was wearing them. She must have big feet."

"She did have socks on. Bruce, you said there were wear patterns on the boots that left those prints on the workbench at Buddy's Place and that the lab would be able to match those if we found the exact boots, correct?"

"Yes. If these," he pointed down to the evidence bag, "are the same boots, we can confirm without question."

"How long will that take?"

"If I drive them down tonight, shouldn't take more than a day or two. Depends what else is on the schedule. They had a couple shootings in Forest County so the guys are pretty busy. You know I'll do my best to speed up the process."

He tweaked an eyebrow as he looked over at her. "Especially if I will need to drive this evidence package back up here . . . a little more help with my double-haul?" Lew punched him in the shoulder before pulling up a chair.

"Mind if I sit here for a few minutes and watch you two eat? I've been running around like a chicken with its head cut off for the last hour."

"Of course not," said Bruce, chewing. He set down his fork. "I have to say I am sorry to hear these are Karen Wright's boots. She seemed like a nice woman."

The mournful expression on his face said it all: Could the universe have let forensic expert Bruce Peters down? As talented as he was in his field, he hated to learn he might be a poor judge of character.

"Grandpa, I am so tired," said Mason walking into Osborne's house and throwing herself onto the living room sofa.

"I am not surprised, young lady. It's almost ten o'clock and neither one of us got much sleep last night, did we? How did your team do? Catch any muskies?" He knew the boys had had a pretty good day up to lunchtime but they weren't sure how close they were to the top of the rankings.

"Got two smaller ones tonight," said Mason.

"No Buster?"

"C'mon, Grandpa." She grinned sheepishly. "Don't make me feel bad about losing that fish."

"Mason, honey, if that's the only fish you ever lose . . . I can't tell you how many fish I've lost over the years. Dozens, maybe hundreds. I don't know a fisherman who hasn't lost a big one. That's what makes it fun."

"Well, okay," she said with a heavy sigh, punching at one of the sofa pillows beside her. "Grandpa, can I go to bed now?" Osborne could see her eyes were closing.

"No ice cream?"

"Oh, for sure." She jumped up. "Then I'll go to bed."

In the middle of the night a sound woke Osborne. He had deliberately left the door to his bedroom open in case Mason needed anything. The sound . . . could it have been a whimper? Maybe a critter snuffling around outside his open bedroom window? He lay listening but the house was quiet. Mike didn't stir from his dog bed. Osborne fell back asleep.

At four forty-five the next morning, he had oatmeal with brown sugar and blueberry muffins set out on the kitchen table. On this, the last morning of the tournament, the fishing would start at six A.M. and end at ten A.M. Mason had told him she needed to be at Ray's by five to be sure everything was ready.

"Hey, sleepyhead," he called downstairs. He had to smile at how Mason's presence in the downstairs bedroom reminded him of how much fun he had had with Erin when she was the same age: two tomboys one generation apart.

After walking Mason down to Ray's, he went back and tried to nap on the sofa but that wasn't going to happen. Giving up, he put Mike on the leash and took a stroll down past the other houses and cottages lining the road to his place. At last it was time for his daily chat with his coffee buddies.

A quick check with Lew after leaving McDonald's found her up to her ears in paperwork. "Still waiting for any news from Bruce on those boots, Doc. Are you free later? I could use your help if I have to make an arrest—"

Osborne nodded before she could finish. "Of course, but I'm going to hope the Wausau boys are wrong on this one."

"Can't argue with circumstantial evidence, and there's no one to confirm where she was that night. Unless she can come up with a witness, I won't have a choice."

"True. Much as I regret it, I guess I have to agree with you on that one," said Osborne. "But on a happier note, Lewellyn, I will have my house back to myself this evening. Can I entice you to join me for one of my gourmet meals? Bill Oliver stopped by with a stringer of bluegills this morning and I thought a little mac 'n' cheese might set those off nicely."

Lew grinned up at him. "Sounds like a plan to me. By the way, how did Ray and the boys do in the tournament?"

"Haven't heard yet." He checked his watch. "I gotta hustle home. Mason should be finishing up and back at my place any minute."

"Grandpa, they came in fifth! Ryan and Jake won fifteen hundred dollars. Can you believe it? And Ray wants me to work with them next summer, too. But, Grandpa, look what Ray paid me." She held out two twenties and a ten. "Fifty bucks. This is the most money I ever made."

"For that kind of money, I hope you helped Ray clean up and put everything away."

"I did, I did," she said, bouncing up and down. Osborne suspected Ray felt guilty about her harrowing adventure in the fishing kayak. He would have to reassure his neighbor Mason's close call was not his fault.

"You know, Grandpa, I love all those tools and lures and stuff that Ray has. Maybe I'll grow up and run a bait shop someday. That stuff is so much fun."

"You should talk to Chief Ferris about that. She worked in her grandfather's sporting-goods store when she was a girl. But settle down now and get your things together, kiddo. Time for me to run you home."

After dropping Mason home, Osborne mulled over her remarks about working for Ray. So she loves tools and lures, does she? He smiled to himself. Maybe she'd like to grow up and be a dentist. Lots of tools in that line of work.

"Do you think Mason might like to try fly-fishing?" asked Lew as she helped Osborne put the dinner dishes in the dishwasher. Osborne had told her how excited Mason had been helping with the tournament. "If she enjoys being around the lures and fishing rods, she might. I have a fly rod she can try."

"And I bought her state-of-the-art waders," said Osborne. "We'll have to take her fly-fishing with us when your schedule has settled down. Any news from Bruce on those hiking boots?"

"Not yet. May have to wait over the weekend," said Lew.

After finishing the dishes they decided to walk down to the dock and settle in to count ducklings as they glided behind the mother duck, who was serene as ever in spite of the squabbling of her offspring.

"Oh, oh, looks like we're down to eight," said Osborne. As he gave Lew a rueful smile a dragonfly with wings of molten gold landed on the rim of her glass of iced tea.

Osborne leaned back on the chaise longue, feet up and an iced coffee in hand. It was the finest of summer evenings as swirls of peach overhead bloomed in pools on the water.

Hours later the two of them, nestled together and sleeping soundly, woke to the ringing of the phone on the bedside table. The sound pierced the quiet night, shrill as a scream.

Chapter Twenty-Four

"Dad, I am so sorry to wake you up but Mason just had the worst nightmare. She is hysterical. But maybe it's not a nightmare." Erin was talking so fast he wasn't sure he heard her correctly.

"Slow down, Erin. Please start over. I'm having a hard time hearing you."

"Dad, it's Mason." Osborne could hear Erin trying to get a grip on herself. "She has had a horrible nightmare. Something awful must have happened to her the other night. Mark said to call. We need your help."

"What time is it?" Osborne struggled to wake up. "Erin, it's two thirty in the morning."

"I know, I know—but she woke up screaming that someone's going to die. I can't settle her down. Mark can't either. She is screaming for the police—"

"I heard that," Lew said in a whisper as she leaned over Osborne's shoulder. "Tell Erin we'll be right there."

Lew was up and pulling on sweatpants and a sweatshirt before Osborne was even out of bed. "We better take your car, Doc. This isn't police business."

Ten minutes later they were on Erin and Mark's front porch. Erin answered the door in her pajamas. "I can't thank you enough for doing this," she said as Lew and Osborne ran by her. "Mason's in the family room with Mark."

Mason was sitting on the sofa with her father's arm around her. The child was trembling. "Chief Ferris, she calmed down a bit when we told her you were coming," said Mark.

"Let me take over," said Lew and sat down beside Mason. She put a hand on Mason's knee. "Okay, young lady, start at the beginning and tell me what it is. But first, take a deep breath. We're all here to listen and I'm sure we can fix it whatever it is."

"I saw the pictures of how they're going to die," said Mason. "See, when I was lost I found this cabin like Dad's hunting shack and I pushed a door open. It wasn't locked." She took a broken breath.

"That's okay, I'm not worried about that," said Lew.

"So I was going to just sleep a little, then try to go home but it was so dark. I . . . um . . . turned on some lights and found this other room." Lew could feel the child's body shaking. "There were pictures on the wall of real people with knives and guns pointing at them."

"Those are posters people use for target practice, honey. Those aren't real."

Mason turned frightened eyes up to Lew and said, "No, they aren't for target practice. I saw the people in real life. I saw how it will happen. They are going to die if we don't find them.

"We have to tell them to be careful. I am so scared because . . ." She burst into tears, her breath catching. ". . . because the bad person will know what I saw and come after me too. Come after me so I won't tell."

"Now, now, I don't think so," said Lew, patting Mason's shoulder in an attempt to calm her down. It wasn't working.

"No one's coming after you," said Mason's parents in unison.

"You're imagining things, honey," said Erin. She glanced over at Lew and Osborne. "I wonder if what she saw was just some idiot's porno collection. Snuff porno. Something like that."

Osborne had felt a chill when Mason was describing what she had seen. It didn't make sense but still . . . Early as it was, he knew he had to make a phone call.

"Ray, sorry to wake you up but we've got a problem. Maybe you can help." After telling him of Mason's terror, he said, "I'm afraid the only way we can help this child is to find that cabin. Find the damn place and show her there is nothing to be afraid of."

"We should do that right now," said Ray. "I'll grab my maps and plat book and be over in minutes. You're at Erin's?"

Twenty minutes later, the adults and Mason gathered around the dining room table as Ray first laid out a fishing map of Loon Lake. They kept their voices low as the other two children were still sleeping soundly.

"Problem I had when we were looking for her the other night," said Ray as he moved a pointer across the map, "is all these inlets along here. I couldn't figure out which was the one she was pulled into."

"The one I was in had a culvert," said Mason. "That's why I got out of the kayak."

"That helps," said Ray. "Narrows our choice to one of three: here, here, and here." Everyone stared at the snake-like lines marking the inlets. "What else do you remember, Mason?"

"Telephone poles."

"Okay, more than likely they were utility poles for power lines," said Ray, opening the plat book. "And you found your way through woods and potato fields to Herm Jensen's place?"

"Yes." Mason had calmed though Osborne could see she was still experiencing bouts of trembling. Gosh, he hoped they could figure this out. Poor kid.

Ray circled an area. "Has to be right in here. According to my plat book the last deed registered for this section indicates ownership by the Wright family trust. I'll bet she found one of the Wright family's old hunting shacks. Let's go, folks."

"Ray, it's four o'clock in the morning," offered Erin. "Shouldn't we wait for dawn at least?"

"Hell, no, this is what adventure is all about, right, Mason?" Ray kidded Mason with a gentle elbow in her ribs, but the look he gave Lew was serious. "What do you think, Chief?"

"Now, we go right now," said Lew. She didn't add that Mason's story had worried her, too. "But, Ray, how old is your plat book?"

"'Bout five years. I don't know that there's been an update published since."

"All right, here's what we do," said Lew. "I want Doc to drive me back to his place so I can change clothes and get my cruiser. We'll meet everyone back here in half an hour. Mason, you're coming, too, so you need to get dressed. Is that okay with everyone?"

"Someone needs to stay here with Beth and Cody," said Mark. "That'll be me. The rest of you go."

Soon there was a caravan driving along the town road that ran between Loon Lake and the potato fields. Ray and Osborne in Ray's pickup led the group, followed by Lew in her cruiser. Erin and Mason in their family Jeep took up the rear.

Twice Ray turned down roads with fire numbers that turned out to be dead ends: one ended in an empty lot where someone was storing firewood; another at an ancient brick house with its windows boarded up and a fallen-down barn. The third road wound deep into a heavily wooded area before emerging into a clearing with a stack of firewood on one side and a cabin so old its logs had turned black.

Ray pulled up and parked. He and Osborne got out and waited for the others to arrive. The sky was lightening and the air cool and crisp as the other vehicles pulled into the clearing.

"What do you think, Mason? Could this be it?"

"Not sure," said Mason. "I know I left the front door unlocked when I left. But I don't want to go in there." She cowered against her mother.

"I'll go first," said Lew, one hand resting on the SIG Sauer at her hip. Ray and Osborne followed several feet behind. The door pushed open easily. It was unlocked.

"Hello?" Lew called. No answer. She walked into the cabin.

Based on what Mason had said earlier, Lew was pretty sure this had to be the one: a small living area with a beat-up old sofa and a wooden rocking chair in front of a fireplace built of river rock. An ancient floor lamp with a stained lampshade stood behind the sofa.

Lew pulled a chain and the lamp turned on. "Got electricity," she said.

Ray walked into the kitchen area, looked around, opened the refrigerator, and came out. "Nothing much here," he said, "but the fridge is on and there's a couple beers in there." He turned on the kitchen tap and water came out. "Whoever it is has the water pump running. I'd say somebody's been in the place recently."

Osborne walked over to a closed door next to a small bathroom and turned the knob. The door opened. He reached in, hoping for a wall switch just inside the door and found one. He flicked it on. To his right, plastered across the wall were the images that had frightened his granddaughter.

They were not pornographic; they were worse. And he recognized the victims.

Lew took one look and grabbed her cell phone. "What did you say the fire number is on this road?" she asked Ray.

"Four-two-one-five."

She repeated the number to the dispatch operator. "I need the name, address, and phone number for the owner of this property ASAP," she said and clicked off.

The three of them studied the five-by-seven-inch color photos on the wall. The subject was familiar: Tiffany Niedermeier. The subject was clothed in some photos, unclothed in others.

Above each was pinned a handwritten note detailing what Osborne assumed were statements made to the photographer by the subject. Each note contained a nasty remark highlighted with quote marks, though each was different. The responses from the photographer were visceral.

Alongside each photo and note was pinned an identical photo but this time a weapon had been taped onto the subject. There were seven original photos, seven duplicates. Most often the weapons taped to scenes were knives or guns, except for the last two photos.

The last photo featured two people: Tiffany and a partner on a piano. No note. The duplicate photo held no weapon: just a large black X.

"Whoever took these was stalking Tiffany," said Lew. "They had cameras rigged in the women's dressing room and bathroom at Buddy's Place, the Deer Creek fitness center, even her bedroom and bath in Deer Creek's barracks for summer employees.

"That last photo must have been taken from that back stairway in the Entertainment Center at Buddy's Place. Tiffany and her partner were so engaged, not to mention drunk—they never knew they were being watched."

After reading the quotes pinned over the photos, Ray asked, "Do you think that woman really said those things? I can't imagine anyone being so downright mean. I wouldn't talk that way to a rock."

"Doesn't surprise me," said Lew. "Based on what Doc and I've been told, she was a master of cruelty and perceptive when it came to choosing her targets. The woman had a sixth sense for picking on people who had been abused before.

"Both Joyce and Nina said they experienced abusive behavior from her but they pushed back. Whoever took these photos seems to be someone Tiffany was torturing. Verbally, that is. But that can be dangerous. You can push a person too far. Just . . . too . . . far."

Lew heaved a sigh. "Mason's instinct was right: someone was going to die. The hard part will be trying to explain to her why and why her warning has come too late. Doc, I think you and Erin need to handle that right now. I do not want that child feeling guilty over this—"

Her cell phone rang. "Yes, we have an owner? Thank you, good work."

Lew looked at Osborne and Ray. "Fred Smith. He's owned this property for a year. Bought it from the family trust. I imagine it was Chet who sold it to him."

"Doc, Ray, you stay with Erin and Mason, please. No reason for anyone to remain out here. Meantime, I want to arrest Fred Smith as soon as possible. I'll have Officer Adamczak meet me at Deer Creek for backup. We know Fred has been living in the caretaker cottage there."

"Wait, Chief Ferris—" Ray started to protest.

"Lewellyn—"Osborne joined him.

"No, you two stay out of this," said Lew. "I don't need anyone else getting hurt." She checked the time. "The sooner Roger and I get there, the better. We can catch him by surprise."

Walking outside where the morning sun was peeking over the pines to the east, Lew strode over to the car where Erin and Mason were waiting. "Mason, this has been very, very helpful. We know who put those pictures up and I am on my way now to arrest him. He cannot hurt you."

Mason raised questioning eyes to Lew. "I'm safe?"

"Very safe. You do not have to worry."

"But those people—are they safe?"

"I have to check on that," said Lew, catching Erin's eye with a silent warning. "I will tell you later. Feel better now, okay?"

Mason nodded as she whispered, "Yes."

Chapter Twenty-Five

Lew pulled into the parking lot in front of the lodge at the Deer Creek Preserve. It was a few minutes before six A.M. She waited until Roger's squad car arrived to park alongside. Climbing out of her cruiser, she motioned for him to follow her.

The front door was open, which surprised Lew, but once inside she saw lights on in Ty Wallis' office. "Good morning, Ty," she said after rapping her knuckles on his open door. "What are you doing here so early?"

Ty looked up from his desk. He did a double-take then grinned. "Hey, if I don't start at six, Chief Ferris, I can't get anything done. All the excitement over at Buddy's Place hasn't made my job easier either." He paused with a sheepish expression on his face. "Truth is I don't sleep that great these days, so might as well get something done.

"Might I ask you the same question? Awfully early for a visit isn't it?"

"I'm here on police business, Ty. Where will I find the caretaker's cottage? That's where Fred Smith is living, correct?"

"He was. Fact is, you are just in time. He's moving out this morning. I fired him last night. He walked in here demanding I let Joyce go but, hell, that woman is the one who does all the heavy lifting around here. Only reason Fred had his job is the Wrights insisted I hire him, but with Chet gone . . ."

Ty stood with a wave of his hand saying, "You don't need to hear all this. I promised the guy a good reference, though. Hell, an excellent recommendation—can't get him out of here fast enough."

"So which way to . . . ?"

"Take a right out the front door and around the building. You'll see a storage shed and the caretaker cottage is right behind that. Holler if you need any help."

Minutes later, Lew and Roger walked past a white golf cart parked in front of the cottage and up to the front door. Lew knocked, saying, "Loon Lake Police, Fred. Please open up."

"Hold on, be right there," said a voice from inside. Lew and Roger stood back, hands on their holstered weapons, ready.

The door opened and Fred stood there half-dressed as he tried stuffing a green work shirt into his pants. "Chief Ferris? Officer Adamczak?"

A quick check of the man in the doorway and Lew was confident he was unarmed. "Fred Smith, I have probable cause to arrest you for the murders of Chet Wright and Tiffany Niedermeier." She started to read him his rights but Fred stopped her. "No need for that."

He backed into the cottage and Lew followed with Roger standing behind her. The room was small but comfortable with knotty pine paneling and cheerful red-and-white curtains at the windows. "Before you handcuff me, can I ask how you know it was me?"

"We found the photos in that hunting shack of yours. Someone got in there by accident the other day, saw them, and alerted us."

"I see."

Lew was struck by how resigned the man seemed. "You did push the lever to raise that piano, didn't you?" Fred nodded.

"Yep. Kind of weird, I guess, but I felt so bad for Karen. She's a beautiful person and she didn't deserve what those two were up to." If a grown man could pout, Fred did as he spat out, "She sure didn't deserve Chet and all that horrible man's BS. Good riddance is what I say."

"Did Karen ask you to . . . take care of things?"

"KayKay? God, no. She's an angel. My angel." Fred's eyes took on a distant look. His voice was calm, soft even. Though he stood in front of her, Lew had the sense he'd left the room. "My guardian angel," he whispered.

"KayKay would never do something like that. Never. But Chet, he hurt her in so many ways, someone had to do something. If it had to be me, I'm all right with that. I am all right with that. She saved my life, see—and I've had the chance to save hers. Right?"

He smiled.

Lew was struck by how calm he was. So calm she wondered if he thought he was going to get away with it. She tensed, ready for him to rush her. But he just kept talking.

"No, no, no. KayKay had no idea what I was planning. But I knew that Chet had a thing about being on the piano with that witch of a woman so I decided it would be a good way for both of them to go. She's the one I really wanted to, um, finish off. At least I hoped that's how it would work."

Watching him as he spoke, Lew saw no remorse in the man's eyes. "Problem was I couldn't be sure they wouldn't see what was happening and stop the piano."

"But you did plan ahead?"

"I guess you can say that. I knew they got together a couple nights a week after hours. Drinking, fooling around, silly jukebox blaring. Couple times I walked in on 'em, they never noticed. The other night I forgot my toolkit and went back late to get it. One of the bathrooms had backed up that afternoon, see, so I had been there earlier. When I saw what they were up to—figured it was good a time as any and pushed the lever."

"What if they hadn't been killed?"

"They would have thought one of them had pulled it. Chet did it once for a prank. You can stop it at the top if you aren't drunk out of your mind, see. Kinda their own fault, is my thinking."

"Well, we'll talk more at the station. Officer Adamczak, would you please cuff Mr. Smith?"

"Excuse me, Chief Ferris, before he does that may I get my wallet out of my dresser in the bedroom? And my medications?"

"Yes, but I have to watch you," said Lew, following him through the door to the bedroom. A black duffel bag stood open on the carefully made bed and she could see he had begun to pack items of clothing.

Fred walked over to an old wooden dresser and pulled open the top drawer. He reached in for a small wooden box and set it on top of the dresser. His back to Lew, he tipped up the lid and reached into the box.

She never saw the gun. He kept his head still and arm movement to a minimum while pulling it from the box and pressing the barrel against the roof of his mouth before pulling the trigger.

The box—a balsa wood cigar box onto which had been burned the words *Baccarat Havana Selection*—wasn't all that Fred had stolen. Checking its contents later that day, Lew found it held a tube of lipstick, one rhinestone drop earring, a black lace thong, a small pipe used for smoking dope, and, of course, the handgun.

The gun was a Charter Arms Cougar Undercover Lite registered to a Tiffany Niedermeier. It had cost its owner $400.

Tiffany had been right on one count: someone had indeed been riffling through her stuff. But she was wrong on the others: the culprit was neither Joyce nor Nina.

Late that afternoon Lew was deep into the paperwork required by the circumstances surrounding Fred Smith's death when her phone rang. She looked up from the computer screen, relieved to have a break for whatever reason.

It was the receptionist at the station's front desk. "Chief Ferris, there is a woman here asking to see you immediately. She said you'd understand why. Her name is Karen Wright." Lew could tell from the warning in the receptionist's voice that Karen was upset.

"Is there someone who can walk her down to my office, please?" asked Lew. "She may be quite emotional."

"Yes, Chief, I'll bring her down."

"Ty Wallis called me with the terrible news," said Karen, eyes stricken. "What on earth? What did you say to Fred? How could you let this happen?" She choked back tears.

"Karen, sit down." Lew walked her over to one of the chairs by the window. "Can I get you a glass of water? A cup of coffee?"

As Karen shook her head and blew her nose, Lew outlined how the day had begun, from Mason's hysteria to the search ending at Fred's hunting shack. "I know the place. We sold it to him. But I can't believe what you're telling me Fred did."

"I know you loved him like a brother," said Lew, "but did you have any idea how fragile his emotional state might be?" Karen sobbed quietly. Then she lifted her head.

"Who knew it would come to this? But . . . one thing doesn't surprise me. Fred hated his mother. He never forgave her for leaving him alone the day the house exploded, not to mention all the other days.

"He shared with me once that she had told him she wished he'd never been born. He was a mistake, she told him. Can you believe that's how Fred's mother treated him? Frankly"—Karen tried talking while blowing her nose—"frankly, Fred was such a runt growing up lots of people picked on him. Tiffany must have got mixed up in his head with those feelings toward his mom. I'm sure that's what happened."

"Tiffany Niedermeier was not discriminating," said Lew. "She was rude, critical, accusative, and nasty to everyone around her—"

"Except Chet."

"Right, except Chet."

"She knew how to handle men okay unless they were of no use to her. Fred did tell me right after he started working for Ty at the preserve that he thought she was trying to get him fired."

"Karen," said Lew, "something we are taught during our training for handling violent domestic abuse situations is that a quarrel may appear to be over something small. But if it triggers a memory from childhood, whether it's feelings of competition, favoritism, power, or lack of power, the reaction can be way bigger than the actual harm done to a person.

"What you might call 'the old stuff' is so poisonous, it can be very, very dangerous. That may be why Tiffany triggered such rage in Fred."

"That makes sense, I guess." Karen was visibly calmer than when she had walked in.

Lew gave a rueful laugh. "It makes more sense than what I have been thinking. Until this morning I mistakenly assumed it was your husband whom the murderer was after and that Tiffany was collateral damage."

"Are you saying you thought it was me?" Karen's eyes opened wide and she sat up straight.

"Five million dollars is a motive. Then there are your boots."

"What about the boots? You mean the ones I borrowed yesterday? From Fred?"

"Yes, we found evidence of an intruder the night that Chet and Tiffany were crushed to death. The individual pushed open a back window of the building and climbed onto a workbench in front of the window. From there they had an excellent view of the piano and the bodies.

"They didn't go any further into the club but they left behind a distinctive set of muddy footprints, which were identified by the crime lab as having been made by a pair of Vasque hiking boots—identical to the boots you were wearing yesterday. Even the wear patterns on the soles match. Got the report from the crime lab a short time ago."

"I borrowed those boots from Fred early Wednesday morning when I knew I would be walking through the swamp to the heron rookery. They were so big I had to wear extra socks."

"Why didn't you tell me that when I came to your house with the search warrant?"

"You didn't ask."

A short time later, as they were walking out of Lew's office, Karen paused to ask, "Chief Ferris, will you let me know when Fred's body will be released from the morgue? Over all the years I've known Fred, he has always been there for me, always ready to help however he could. He was odd but I loved him.

"I consider myself his family and I want to bury him. In spite of all that has happened, my friend deserves that respect."

Chapter Twenty-Six

The sidewalk was slick from a light rain as Osborne walked from McDonald's to Lew's office. Even though he had downed three cups of black coffee with his buddies he was hoping for one final splash of caffeine with Police Chief Lewellyn Ferris.

"Quiet this morning, Lewellyn?" he asked, peering around the door to her office.

Lew looked up from her desk, eyes happy to see him. "It is, believe it or not. Come on in, Doc. Made plenty of coffee this morning."

"You look more relaxed than you have in weeks." And lovely as ever, Osborne wanted to add, but he knew that would irritate her.

Though the summer police uniform of khaki shirt and pants couldn't hide the curve of her breasts, the rest of Lewellyn Ferris was no-nonsense. Sturdy, wide-shouldered, and generously hipped, she preferred not to be reminded she was a woman in what too many locals still considered a man's job.

"Sit down, won't you, Doc? Karen Wright is due here any minute to answer a few final questions. You might be interested in what she has to say, and please don't hesitate to jump in if you have questions. You're still a deputy on this case."

"The boys at McDonald's are surprised there'll be no memorial service for Chet," said Osborne. "Mick Madson from the funeral home is a little put out about that. Between casket, flowers, and a luncheon he had been expecting to make a bundle."

"Really? I think Karen made the right decision," said Lew. "Cremation and a private burial in the family plot: end of a sad story. Wouldn't you agree?"

A gentle knock on the open door to Lew's office and Karen poked her head in. "Am I interrupting?"

"Not at all. Please come in," said Lew. "Can Doc pour you a cup of coffee?"

"Yes, please. With a touch of cream?" She smiled as she sat down and accepted the coffee mug that Osborne handed her.

Once Lew had finished going over the remaining legalities, Karen said, "You may appreciate knowing that thanks to a speedy payment from the life insurance company and help from my accountant, I will be able to pay off most of Chet's debts. That includes paying back what Chet had overbilled Bert, Jud, and Pete at the club."

"Overbilled? That's an interesting way to put it," said Lew. "Makes Chet's misbehaving sound less onerous, more like he just made a few bookkeeping errors."

"My accountant made the suggestion," said Karen. "I will have my lawyer review it but if I can do that, it will save me months, if not years, of wrangling with lawyers, banks, and credit card companies. I would rather pay the money and have it out of my life.

"Just as important, those three men will be happy and stop bothering me. Although, Dr. Osborne, remember how you asked about my relationship with Pete Kretzler? That got me thinking. Especially as he has stopped by my house two more times recently." She narrowed her eyes as she spoke.

"Consoling the wealthy widow?" asked Lew, leaning back in her chair.

"You got it. Chief Ferris, I think you and I would make good friends," said Karen with a chuckle. "Yes, he's 'overshared' the travails of his marriage and I know he thinks I'm worth five million bucks."

Glee crossed Karen's face as she said, "Just wait until I tell him all that's left is enough for me to pay for two years of grad school and a rental down in Wausau. Plus the premiums on the five-million-dollar insurance policy for me are so high that I've canceled it. How often do you think he's going to stop by once he knows that?

"If I've learned anything over these years of being related by marriage to people of great wealth, it's this: Money does not make any man—or woman—a better human being. That includes my late husband and his three less than honorable friends. I don't mean to sound bitter, but keeping that in mind is a reality check that is helping me get through this."

Her eyes turned sad as she said, "What I can't change is how bad I feel about Fred. It was our fault, Chet's and mine, that he ended up having to work at the preserve and around that—"

"Karen, stop right there," said Osborne. "The average person would never have reacted to Tiffany Niedermeier's nastiness like Fred did. His rage came from somewhere deep and dark in his childhood. Please, you need to consider the good years he had thanks to you."

"Thanks for saying that," said Karen as she got to her feet. "You make me feel a little better. And thank you for the coffee, Chief Ferris. If there are more questions from the lawyers as I work on settling Chet's estate, I may have to give you a call. Hope you don't mind."

"Of course not," said Lew, standing up. "Comes with the job."

"Oh—I have one last question myself." Karen hesitated in the doorway. "It's about those hiking boots. If you had not learned that it was Fred who pulled the lever hoisting the piano that night and all you had to work with were the footprints from boots you knew I had worn—could I have been convicted of murder based on circumstantial evidence?"

"No," said Lew. "There was dried sweat in those boots that indicated more than one person had worn them. Thank advances in DNA testing for that. Once it was determined that those were the exact boots that left the muddy footprints on the workbench, Bruce Peters had the boot interiors tested, too. The test results confirmed a match between the sweat in the boots and Fred Smith's DNA.

"Added to that were the photos Ray Pradt took of the tracks made by the golf cart Fred used. Those matched as well. I'm sure we would have found more evidence linking Fred to the murders if we had had to continue the investigation."

It was five o'clock when Lew's fishing truck pulled into Osborne's driveway. Erin's Jeep was close behind. Throwing open the door of her mother's car, Mason leapt from the front seat shouting, "Chief Ferris, hey, Grandpa said you have a fishing rod for me?"

"Mason, hey," said Lew, mimicking her with a big grin as she climbed out of her truck. "To answer your question, I have a *fly* rod for you to try. Not a fishing rod, but a fly rod, the kind used for fly-fishing. You'll see there's a difference. Now hustle inside and let your grandfather know his dates for the evening have arrived."

"O-k-a-a-y." Calling over her shoulder, Mason raced for Osborne's back door. When she had disappeared inside, Lew walked over to where Erin was backing her car around to leave and motioned for her to lower her window.

"How's Mason doing, Erin? Any more nightmares?"

"Not so far, thank goodness. We followed your advice, Chief Ferris, and Mark and I told her the whole story. How a person whom she doesn't know and never will was picked on so often during his life that he became so angry he killed someone.

"We assured her she was right to feel that something bad was going to happen. But we said over and over that the person who owned the cabin, that the person who put up the pictures—that person was dead now and could never ever hurt her."

Erin rolled her eyes. "Sometimes I worry we let our kids watch too much TV. Where she got the idea that she was a witness to a crime and would have to be killed is beyond me but that is what was in her head. You may think we told her too much but it seems to be working."

"Thank goodness," said Lew. "I am no child psychologist but I believe in parents being as honest and open as possible. It's not knowing the truth that can scare a kid."

"Well, we kept it pretty real."

Erin smiled as she said, "She is pretty darn excited today. Very nice of you to take the time to show her how to cast. I know how busy you are, Chief Ferris.

"Mark heard that Trout Unlimited will be holding a two-day kids fly-fishing camp next month where members will show them how to cast, how to tie trout flies, how to identify insects, and lots of other fly-fishing stuff, so we've signed her up for that, too."

"Great. We'll get her started today. At least she'll know what a fly rod looks like."

"Sounds fun. Will you let Dad know I'll be back at eight to pick her up?"

"Sure." With a wave, Erin drove off.

Half an hour later, Lew and Mason had taken over Osborne's backyard. Sitting on the stoop in front of his back door, Mike panting happily beside him, Osborne watched as Lew demonstrated for Mason the basic mechanics of the back cast, the power snap, and the forward cast. Then she had Mason try each move.

"Very good," said Lew after half a dozen attempts by the eleven-year-old. "But that's enough up here on the grass. Let's go down to the lake."

"Really? Really?" Mason jumped up and down. "Think I'll catch a fish?"

"Maybe not quite yet," said Lew with a wink at Osborne. "Fly-fishing takes practice but you seem to have a knack for it." Then she added the words of encouragement she always used on Osborne and Bruce when they were flailing away: "You may not be expert yet but you will catch fish."

"Say, Doc," said Lew walking over to where he was sitting. "Let's have Mason pull on those waders you bought her and we'll continue this lesson down in the water. While she gets changed, I'm going to walk over to Ray's and borrow that fishing kayak. I'm curious to see how it works."

Ten minutes later, Lew came paddling around the bend in the shoreline between Osborne and Ray's properties. She glided soundlessly to within a few feet of Osborne's dock. Mason was standing on the beach and waiting for instruction before wading in.

"Nice waders," said Lew, scrutinizing her garb. "I like those wading boots."

"Glad you approve," said Osborne from the dock. "They weren't cheap."

"I'm sure not," said Lew. "Next time the city gives me a raise, I'll get myself a pair of waders just like those. Mine have holes beyond patching."

Osborne made a mental note to surprise a certain someone on her birthday. After all, since he'd felt like he was going broke spending $500 on his granddaughter, why not empty the bank account and spend $500 more on his favorite fly-fisherman? What's the old saying? You can't take it with you.

Coaching from the kayak, Lew got Mason into the water waist high. After having her go through the motions of casting for a good half hour, she said, "That's enough for now. You're off to a good start, Mason.

"Before I paddle back to Ray's, I want to tell you something important. This kayak is made for fishing smaller fish like trout or bass or walleye. *Not muskies.* Even a small muskie can be long enough and weigh enough to make fishing from here difficult.

"This kayak might skim beautifully across the water, but it doesn't have the weight to counter the pull, much less the attack, of a big fish. I can't believe you held on to Buster as long you did without hurting yourself. You are a brave girl."

Mason blushed, grinning with pride.

After midnight, Osborne heard the wind pick up. He got out of bed and ran to the porch to close windows before the rain hit. Scrambling back under the summer coverlet, he lay beside Lew. Together they watched the lightning flash as rumbles of thunder grew nearer.

Suddenly with a loud crack and pounding rain, the storm hit with all its fury. Osborne pulled Lew close and she curled into him.

"Isn't it fine," he said, "to feel so safe in a thunderstorm?" He felt her smile in the dark.

Acknowledgments

It is high time I say "thank you" to the hard-working professionals who have helped *Dead Loudmouth*, the sixteenth book in my Loon Lake Mystery series, find its way to mystery-loving readers.

A first thank-you goes to my agent, Martha Millard, who is with Sterling Lord Literistic, Inc. Over the years she has always been there for me with advice and encouragement whether I was writing nonfiction or fiction. Her instincts have proven to be impeccable and she is one tough negotiator. I have been fortunate to be among her clients.

My publisher, Ben LeRoy of Tyrus Books/F+W Media, has been a true friend and champion of this author. Insightful, innovative, and intrepid—Ben has not hesitated to challenge a marketplace too often overshadowed by mega-publishers. I have been lucky to have Ben in my corner as he has built Tyrus Books into a publishing house highly respected in the competitive field of crime fiction.

But it is the editorial talents of Ashley Myers and her predecessor, Alison Dasho, who have fine-tuned my rough copy and provided the guidance that has helped to make the words sing. And thanks, too, for the unswerving attention to detail provided by Tyrus Books' expert copyeditor, Heather Padgen.

First impressions count and I am grateful for the lovely, haunting jacket design provided by Stephanie Hannus. A final thank-you goes to Bethany Carland-Adams, whose excellent and indefatigable publicity efforts continue to generate coverage from key reviewers and media nationwide.

A heartfelt thank-you to everyone in my publishing family: You make me look good.

About the Author

Photo credit: Marcha Moore

In her teens and twenties, mystery author Victoria Houston was the classic hometown girl who couldn't wait to leave her small Wisconsin town. She has not only returned to her hometown, Rhinelander, but she has based her popular mystery series in the region's fishing culture.